The Baghdad Eucharist

A NOVEL

SINAN ANTOON

Sinan Antoon is an award-winning poet, novelist, and translator. He was born in Iraq, and moved to the United States in 1991 after the Gulf War. He received his PhD from Harvard University and is currently associate professor of Arabic literature at New York University. He is the author of two collections of poetry and four novels, including *I'jaam*, *The Corpse Washer*, and *Fihris* (The Book of Collateral Damage).

The Baghdad Eucharist (published in Arabic as *Ya Maryam*) was shortlisted for the International Prize for Arabic Fiction in 2013.

Maia Tabet is a literary translator, journalist, and editor, who has translated prominent authors such as Elias Khoury. She was born in Beirut and is currently based in Baltimore in the United States.

*

"Faithfully reproduces the difficult conversations between an Iraqi Christian family housed in Baghdad while the daily scenes of carnage are painfully recounted."   —*The Guardian*

"Antoon seems to just get better and better."   —*The National*

"Sinan Antoon is one of the most talented of the younger generation of Iraqi writers to have emerged from the chaos of that country's recent history."   —*Banipal*

"The first novel to broach the tragedy of Iraqi Christians . . . narrating Iraq's wounds in beautiful language."   —*as-Safir*

"[A] panoramic view of Iraq, its history, its iconography and its bitter present . . . Antoon is fast becoming not only the voice of the disaffections of modern Iraq, but also one of the most acclaimed authors of the Arab world."   —*Al-Ahram Weekly*

"Like a masterful filmmaker, twenty-four hours is all that Antoon needs to present a modern-day Iraqi tragedy in his elegant novel. . . . This is a novel that comes to grips with an explosive topic, yet does so without a loss of artistry."   —*Al Jazeera*

The Baghdad Eucharist

Sinan Antoon

Translated by
Maia Tabet

hoopoe
AN IMPRINT OF AUC PRESS

First published in 2017 by
Hoopoe
113 Sharia Kasr el Aini, Cairo, Egypt
200 Park Ave., Suite 1700 New York, NY 10166
www.hoopoefiction.com

Hoopoe is an imprint of the American University in Cairo Press
www.aucpress.com

Published by arrangement with Rocking Chair Books Ltd and RAYA the agency for Arabic Literature

English translation copyright © 2017 by Maia Tabet

Dar el Kutub No. 14204/16
ISBN 978 977 416 820 8

Dar el Kutub Cataloging-in-Publication Data

Antoon, Sinan
     The Baghdad Eucharist / Sinan Antoon.—Cairo: The American University in Cairo Press, 2017.
        p.   cm.
        ISBN 978 977 416 820 8
        1. Arabic Fiction — Translation into English
        892.73

2 3 4 5   21 20 19 18

Designed by Adam el-Sehemy
Printed in the United States of America

He came unto his own, and his own received him not.
The Gospel according to John, 1:11

Living in the Past

1

"You're just living in the past, Uncle!" Maha burst out as she ran from the living room after our argument. Luay, her husband, was upset and he called out after her, his face flushed.

"Hey, Maha, where are you going? Come back! Maha!" But she was already hurtling up the stairs that led to the second floor. He looked downcast as he apologized.

"Forgive her, Uncle. You know how much she loves and respects you." In a voice speckled with shame, he added, "She's a nervous wreck and can't help herself."

Before I could think of anything to say, the sound of her fitful sobbing reached us from the second floor.

"It's all right. It's no big deal. Go calm her down and comfort her," I muttered.

I was sitting on a chair set smack in front of the television and Maha's husband got up from the gray sofa where they had both been seated and came over to me. Placing his hand on my shoulder, he leaned down and kissed the top of my head.

"I'm really sorry," he said. "I owe you." He turned away and slowly climbed the stairs.

A host and his guest were having a heated discussion on television, and even though I was right up against the screen, their faces were nothing but a blur and I couldn't tell what they were saying, despite their raised voices. All I could hear were the words ringing in my ears, "You're just living in the past, Uncle!"

2

I didn't sleep well that night. I tossed in the dark as Maha's stinging pronouncement played over and over in my head. I kept asking myself whether I really did live in the past, but all I could come up with were further questions. How could someone my age, to some degree or another, *not* live in the past? Being in my seventies, most of my life was behind me and very little of it still lay ahead. She, on the other hand, was in her early twenties and, however gloomy the present may be, she still had her whole future before her. She was kindhearted and meant well but she was only half formed. Just like her past. She too would begin to revisit the past once it had grown a little, and she would dwell on it for hours—even were it to consist of nothing but misery. Her wounds would heal and she would retain only what was best. In any case, for me to stop living in the past, it would have to be dead. And it clearly wasn't—the past was alive and well, in one form or another, and it not only coexisted with the present, but continued to wrangle with it. Perhaps it was just being held captive inside the frames of all the snapshots hanging on the walls of the house, suspended along the mile-long walls of my memory, and lying between the covers of our photo albums? Hadn't she stood before them often enough and asked me to point out different family members and questioned me about what had happened to them, where they were now, how they had died, and when? How often had she asked me to tell her the stories contained within those frames? I had always responded to her questions readily, coloring in the details and following various threads that sometimes led to other photos or to other stories that hadn't been captured by the camera's lens—stories laced with sighs of pleasure or with laughter that were lodged in my memory, and others that were preserved in an archive guarded by my heart.

Was I really escaping the present and seeking refuge in the past, as she alleged? Even if it were true, was there shame in it when the present was no more than a booby-trapped snare full of car bombs, brutality, and horror? Perhaps the past was like the garden which I so loved and which I tended as if it were my own daughter, just in order to escape the noise and ugliness of the world. My own paradise in the heart of hell, my own 'autonomous region' as I sometimes liked to call it. I would do anything to defend that garden, and the house, because they were all I had left. I really had to forgive her. My youth was not her youth, her time and my time were worlds apart. Her green eyes fluttered open to the ravages of war and sanctions; deprivation, violence, and displacement were the first things she tasted in life. I, on the other hand, had lived in prosperous times, which I still remembered and continued to believe were real.

3

I woke at 6:30, as I had done for many years, without the use of an alarm clock. My bladder, which awakened me several times a night, was all the alarm I needed. I washed my face and shaved in front of the mirror in the bathroom by my bedroom, but didn't break out into one of my favorite songs, as was my habit, because I wanted to recapture the details of my dream. I took my dentures out of their glass of water, opened my mouth, and secured them in place. I had lost my teeth years ago, and I eventually grew used to the dentures, despite having found them uncomfortable for a while. I was proud that I still had a full head of thick, albeit white, hair. Anything but baldness!

In the dream, I *had* gone bald and that alone made it feel more like a nightmare. The house had been the same in every particular, except that it was a museum. Each room had become a hall with cordoned-off chairs and beds, and there were signs everywhere warning visitors not to touch or get too close. I was the docent, and as I recounted the history of each room, I explained who had lived there and where they had gone. Although I heard whispering and giggling, the rooms were empty. I went from hall to hall looking for visitors but there was no one around. Then, I heard a voice that belonged to a man who was leading a group of visitors down the hallway but he was giving them faulty information about the house. I went toward them and shouted, "This is *my* house, and I am the docent here." But no one heard me or took any notice. I looked in the mirror and saw that I was bald.

I combed my hair and thanked my lucky stars I still had all of it. I opened my eyes wide and peered into my face in the mirror, raising my thick gray eyebrows slowly and crunching together the wrinkles time had etched onto my brow. I stepped back from the mirror, and dried my face and forehead one last time.

On my way from the bathroom to the kitchen to make tea, I stopped in front of the hallway calendar, just as I had done for years. Even after I had retired and there was no longer any business to attend to or any appointments to keep, I never gave up the habit. I'd stop in the hallway and signal the beginning of a new day by crossing out the previous one on the calendar. I would do this using a pencil that hung by a thread from the nail that held the calendar in place. I looked at the current month's photograph of an empty bench with a few yellowed leaves scattered on the paving stones in front of it; a fall wind had blown the leaves down from a nearby tree, whose trunk alone was visible. Below the photograph, only one day remained, the last day of the month of October 2010, which was a Sunday. "Hinna's passing," I had written into the small square.

Truth be told, I needed no reminder of the day my sister had left us, on a morning like this one seven years ago. I'd been to the church earlier this month to ask the priest to offer a prayer for the repose of her soul on the anniversary of her death, and had agreed to pay an extra tithe. The special service wouldn't be held at the sanctuary where my sister had gone for decades in the convent that had become her second home. Since the convent had closed its doors to worshippers for security reasons, the service would be held at what was popularly known as Umm al-Taq, the Church of Our Lady of Deliverance. It was the church Maha and her husband attended on Sundays because he was a Syriac Catholic. Hinna would not mind that the service was being held there rather than at the Chaldean church, "our church" as she called it. The differences between the two were insignificant: both were Eastern Catholic denominations and the liturgy was almost identical, except for a few words here and there. In the end, the prayers were all addressed to the same God, regardless of language or denomination, and that's what counted.

It had been seven years since that fateful morning. How fast they had gone by! Had she lived to witness them, Hinna would have been incredulous. Not only had they been worse than anything that had come before, they even rivaled the last seven months of Hinna's life, the months that followed the outbreak of the 2003 war.

Hinna always got up before I did and made tea for both of us. Her breakfast was very simple: a piece of bread with a little white or yellow cheese, a spoonful of the apricot or fig jam which she loved and made herself, and two istikans of tea. She would sit the teapot on top of the kettle with the flame of the burner turned all the way down, so that the tea would still be hot when I woke up and was ready to drink it. Then, she would walk to church. Her gait had worsened over the years, she moved slowly and only with the help of a cane. She wouldn't hear of me getting up early to give her a ride nor would she listen when I suggested that she could go to church just on Sundays instead of every day. She was extremely hard-headed, especially when it came to her religious observances.

When I went into the kitchen that morning, I saw that Hinna had not made the tea. The teapot lay upturned on the dish drainer by the sink, just as it had been the previous night after we'd had our evening tea. I assumed she wasn't feeling well, so I filled the kettle, placed it on the right-hand burner, and lit a match under it. I put two generous tablespoons of tea leaves in the teapot, moistened them with a few drops of water, covered the pot and placed it on top of the kettle, and waited for the water to boil before pouring it over the leaves.

I left the kitchen and went down to the end of the hallway toward her room, right by the door that led to the backyard. Her door was shut. I rapped three times, calling her name. "Hinna! Hinna! Hinna, dear . . . ."

No answer. I turned the doorknob gently and opened the door as quietly as I could. She was still in bed. The morning sun streamed through between the gaps of the drawn curtains and from either side. I stepped inside the room, which I rarely entered, and pressed on the light switch to the right of the door. Nothing happened. I remembered her telling me the day before that the bulb had burned out and needed replacing, and although I'd told her that I'd take care of it, I hadn't; I berated myself for having put off fetching the ladder from the storeroom, but my knee would hurt whenever I climbed up to change a bulb. What with all the power outages and trying to save on using the electric generator, I had rationalized that we would just use candles at night. Putting off such things was never a good idea.

I called out once more, "Hinna, what's wrong? Get up! Come on, Hinna!"

I went toward the window on the right, and pushed open the curtains. The sun flooded into the middle of the room. I shielded my eyes from the glare, turned around, and went toward the bed. She was lying on her left side, with the quilt drawn up over her shoulders. Approaching the edge of the bed, I looked at her intently. Her eyes were closed and a few strands of her silvery hair lay matted by her face on the pillow. Her hands, with the rosary wrapped around them, were clasped together at the bottom of the pillow to the right of her face; the rosary never left her and the rhythmical clicking of its tiny red beads accompanied all her prayers and invocations. She must have kissed it before falling asleep because the small silver cross at its tip was still resting on her lips.

I leaned down and shook her shoulder, gently repeating her name, "Hinna, Hinna."

She didn't stir. Her shoulder felt rigid and there was a waxy pallor to the crisscross of wrinkles that mapped her face. "Hinna, Hinna dear," I repeated quietly.

I tried to take her pulse but her clasped hands were entwined in the rosary. My heart sank. She was cold to the touch, and I knew instantly that she would never wake up. I wrapped my fingers around her wrist with the tip of my index against her vein, but the pulsing beat of life was silent.

That night, life gathered its last vestiges and vacated Hinna's body, leaving it to death's undivided attention. The good Lord had granted the wish she had often expressed over the years, at particularly painful or trying times. "Dear God," she would exclaim, "take me to You, and relieve me!" She always wished others a long life but for herself she sought only its curtailment. "No more, Lord. Let me be done!" she would say.

I sat on the edge of the bed. I wanted to embrace her one last time, but just stroked her silvery hair with my left hand. I hardly ever touched or kissed her, maybe once or twice a year on the occasion of a holiday. The last time I remembered stroking her hair was when I was still a child. We had lost our mother, and despite Hinna's tender age, it was to her that fell the task of caring for my younger brothers and me. She was only fifteen when she had to give up her dream of entering the convent, and she devoted the rest of her life to ensuring we were comfortable and had enough to eat. Whatever time was left after discharging her duties she spent in religious devotion, either at home or at church. I released her rigid hand to wipe away the tears that had begun to run down my cheeks. I kissed her cold forehead and said, "Rest in peace, Hinna." I said it out loud, as if she could hear me.

A picture of the Virgin Mary hung above the bed. The holy mother appeared full of grace, holding the fruit of her womb against her robes of blue. A shaft of celestial light pierced the sky above and angels circled around her, wings aflutter. Despite the beatitude of her features, there was a sad cast to the eyes looking down on my sister and me.

The tears flowed as I prayed for Hinna's soul. I intoned, "Our Father who art in heaven," just as she had done for me over the course of an entire lifetime. And I followed that with, "Hail Mary, full of grace. Our Lord is with thee. Blessed art thou among women, and blessed is the fruit of thy womb, Jesus. Holy Mary, Mother of God, pray for us sinners, now and at the hour of our death. Amen."

4

I let go of the pencil. Here was the past coming back to remind me of Hinna, as if I could've forgotten her in the first place. I went toward her room, which I had decided to keep exactly as it had been when she was alive. Except for her clothes, which I had asked one of my nieces to collect from the small closet following the condolence period, the room remained unchanged. Hinna's clothes had gone to the church for distribution to the poor.

I opened the door and stepped inside. The room was cold and dark as a tomb. I turned on the light, the switch was to the right of the door, but it didn't dispel the darkness. Then I remembered that we had no power, and in any case, I had never replaced that burned-out lightbulb. I didn't see the point after Hinna's own light was gone from the room, even when the women attending her came to wash her body, comb her hair, and clothe her in a manner befitting her final journey to the grave. I told the women from the neighborhood and our remaining female relatives in Baghdad that there was sufficient daylight for their purpose and I asked them to keep the room lit with candles throughout the night. I was sure that Maha had closed the curtains the last time she'd cleaned the room because I always left them open. The first time she cleaned Hinna's room, she'd said, "It's like a shrine, Uncle—you can feel her spirit is still there."

I went to the window and drew open the curtains as I had done exactly seven years earlier. A gray dove perching on the far side of the brick ledge flew off toward the neighbors' house. The sun poured in, blanketing part of the floor and two-thirds of the bed, which was covered by a white sheet that Maha had placed over the eiderdown. I took three steps toward the window closest to the bed and drew open those curtains too. Morning enveloped the room. I turned around and stood by the bed, looking at the picture of the Virgin Mary above it. To the left was a photo of my brother, Jamil, who fled Iraq in 1969 after his friend was condemned to death on charges of being a Freemason. Even though Jamil wasn't a Mason, his Lebanese wife feared he would suffer a similar fate and they moved to Lebanon. They had three children, and there were five grandchildren so far. They lived in an area of Beirut called Sinn al-Fil to start with but after their house was destroyed during the civil war, they moved to Bikfaya, close to her parents. He was still in his prime in that photograph. Even though she denied it, Hinna loved him best of all, more than me and all our other siblings. The rest of the room was given over to icons and statuettes and other small votive figurines of the Virgin Mary and Jesus, which Hinna collected. Some of them she had brought back from her last trip with the church to Rome in 1989, after the ban on foreign travel was lifted. I would sometimes needle her and say that her room was a miniature church, but for the lack of incense and an altar.

"With you officiating, no doubt!" she'd retort.

She even had a replica of the small glass filled with holy water that worshippers dipped their forefinger in before crossing themselves and stepping inside the church. The glass stood on a little shelf under the light switch to the right of the door. About half a meter below sat the old Singer treadle sewing machine that she labored on as a seamstress for years until the rest of us began to earn our livings. She'd insisted on keeping it even though it no longer worked and she hadn't used it in decades. The machine's table was another space on which to place small statuary. A wooden wardrobe stood in the corner closest to the Singer and, alongside it, was a dressing table with a large mirror. Except for the medium-sized hairbrush with a tuft of white hair still in it, and a few combs, there was nothing relating to Hinna's physical appearance on the dressing table. It was entirely given over to her spiritual pursuits—a stack of prayer books, which accompanied her throughout her life, and an assortment of small pictures distributed by the church. The size of a greeting card, or slightly smaller, some depicted the Virgin Mary alone, while others were of the Madonna and child, St. Joseph, Mary Magdalene, or other saints. There were also photos marking her loved ones' religious milestones—the christenings and First Communions of nephews and nieces—which she placed among the pictures of saints for their protective powers.

A small wooden coffer in the middle of the dressing table, which I knew she had bought in Italy, contained an assortment of rosaries, and her 'live' gold cross. She wore it around her neck, convinced that it contained a miniscule fragment of the original cross. To the left of the dressing table was a wall covered with photographs of religious potentates: one of a smiling Pope John Paul II in his white papal gowns; below that, a picture of Patriarch Boulos Sheikho II, the head of the world Chaldean congregation, whom she had placed beneath the Roman pontiff even though they were ranked equally; and further down, was Sheikho's successor, whose photo was inscribed with the words, "His Eminence Raphael I Bidawid, Chaldean Catholic Patriarch of Babylon."

Underneath the pictures of the pope and the patriarchs, there was a smaller photo of her in a heavy black coat standing in front of the Holy See. She was forever recalling her pilgrimage to the Vatican. She liked Rome very much but always bemoaned the fate of Jerusalem, which she had visited in 1966. Whenever the subject of Palestine came up in discussions or on television, she would say, "And when will Jerusalem be ours again so we can go to the Holy Sepulcher?"

In addition to countless mementos and pictures, Hinna had come back from Jerusalem bearing two crucifixes. A small one that was tattooed on the underside of her forearm, along with 1966, the year she made the pilgrimage to the Holy Land. That little crucifix went with her to the grave where she rests. The larger one, made of olive wood, still hung on the wall facing the bed, alone and unadorned.

I opened a window to let in some fresh air and decided to leave it open in spite of the cold. As I left the room and closed the door, it occurred to me that Hinna's spirit might be pining for her room and come by for a visit. I would close the window at dusk before heading to the church.

5

As I made the tea, I remembered the heat of my argument with Maha. While she had clearly crossed the limits of mutual respect by the tone she used in her aggressive disparagement of my views, I didn't want her to feel anything but ease at being here, especially as these were the last few months before she and her husband were due to leave the country. Despite my love of solitude and the reclusiveness to which I was accustomed, their presence had restored vitality and a sweet feeling to the vast, stiff-jointed house. Maha and her husband had taken on so many of the burdens associated with running a household: Luay was always ready to offer a helping hand and Maha's cooking was truly excellent. It wasn't comparable to Hinna's of course, but I relished everything she made—I had grown so tired of sandwiches and salads and my limited repertoire of simple dishes.

I sat at the kitchen table sipping my tea and thinking about the best way to ease the tense atmosphere and the bitter taste left by the previous night's argument. I chuckled to myself when it hit me that even from the gloom of their prisons, the Baathists could still cause trouble. I didn't know whether to laugh or cry about the fact that this was the second time that Tariq Aziz had provoked family friction. The first time was in the late 1980s when Hinna and I had had a similarly heated argument after she'd told me that she'd seen Aziz's wife crying in church on Sunday. She attended regularly, my sister said, and she cried throughout the service. It was no doubt because she knew what her husband was up to, I had retorted. To which she objected virulently by saying that he was a God-fearing man who had nothing to do with what the rest of the government was up to. He made generous donations to the church, and had footed the bill for the magnificent new chandeliers hanging from the ceiling. I could see for myself, she chided, if only I would deign to set foot in church. His contributions did not absolve him of responsibility for his history and his actions, I told her, adding that they were paltry in light of the brutal treatment being meted out. And, anyhow, why didn't *he* go to church to pray and do penance for his sins, I asked? I told her that this was a confirmation of the widely circulated rumor that he had converted to Islam, along with Michel Aflaq.

"Oh, really? So why don't you go to church and atone for *your* sins?" she protested indignantly.

"Because I don't have any. At least not ones that cause people any harm."

"What are you saying? That simply not harming people is enough? What about your religious duties?"

I went to church only on special occasions and on holidays. Over the decades, Hinna had given up hope that I would do as enjoined by the Ten Commandments and observe the day of the Lord, and she took advantage of every opportunity to remind me that I was a renegade. I couldn't plead or convince her, albeit in jest, that she was my churchgoing proxy.

"You're praying enough for seven people by going to church every day," I would tell her, "so why not pick another six on whose behalf you could consider yourself to have prayed?"

Whenever I spoke like that, she'd look at me sideways, shake her head, and just clam up.

And now, two decades on, Tariq Aziz, along with several others, had been sentenced to death for his role in executions, purges, and forced displacements. This had happened five days earlier and the airwaves and newspaper columns were full of loud and fierce arguments about the merits of the judgment, given the man's frailty and advanced age and his self-proclaimed innocence. Aziz denied any involvement in the massacres of Kurds and Shiites, and claimed he was a diplomat whose sole responsibility was the conduct of foreign affairs.

The first time I had an argument with Maha and Luay, it hadn't led to a confrontation. She had derided the trial as a mockery of justice—instead of busying themselves with sentencing innocent old men to death, she'd said, they should be giving redress to ordinary people for all the problems they faced. Luay had asked for my opinion, and I'd said that besides the procedural flaws, the courts involved were unconstitutional since they had been set up under the occupation; it would've been better to wait and not act so hastily, I added. Even Saddam shouldn't have been executed, but been left to rot in prison for the rest of his days, I told him. And Tariq Aziz *was* complicit insofar as he knew what the Baathists were up to.

"But aren't they sentencing him to death because he's a Christian?" Maha had shot back, her tone petulant.

"My dear, it's more complicated than who's a Christian and who's a Muslim. The issue is a political one, it has to do with powerful interests, not with religion," I'd replied. Maha hadn't said anything more, but she'd clearly indicated that she didn't like what she'd heard when she slapped her own cheek and covered her mouth as if to suggest that she'd had to stop herself from speaking.

Yesterday, however, she had shown no such restraint. We had revisited the subject after hearing a new development in the story, as we were having tea. The announcer

13

had said that President Jalal Talabani had issued a statement announcing that he would not approve the death sentence and that he respected Tariq Aziz as a Christian. The Vatican had stepped in and was trying to intervene to have him released, added the announcer.

"But isn't it the exact same Dawa Party people who carried out the grenade attack and tried to assassinate him in Mustansiriya in 1979 that are trying to kill him now because he's a Christian?" Maha responded, shaking her head. "Aren't they terrorists too? Is it him or them who should be condemned to death? Under the pretext of the rule of law, these terrorists can now sit in judgment of a public figure of his stature!"

"What rule of law, my dear? They're of a piece, all of them, just criminals and thieves! The 'rule of straw' is what they should call it, not the rule of law."

Then we heard the voice of Tariq Aziz's son in conversation with the announcer over the phone. He said the death sentence was politically motivated and he called for the intervention of the international community to free his father who was innocent and in poor health.

Listening to him, I remembered Aziz's haughty demeanor during press conferences when he'd blow on a Cuban cigar in emulation of his master and leader; I recalled too how he had once threatened a British journalist with death. However, I didn't say anything in order to keep the peace; it was enough, I thought, that the man would spend the rest of his days in jail. But Maha had escalated the argument.

"If he were one of *them* they'd never have handed down a death sentence, but the blood of Christians is cheap!" she exclaimed.

I answered her calmly, "And what about those that were condemned to death before him? Weren't they Muslims? He's the first, and the only, Christian to get a death sentence."

"Don't you see how they're killing us everywhere, without due process, or a word of protest? Churches are being torched, we're being killed right, left, and center, and we are slowly but surely being driven out."

"Maha dear, it's not only churches. Far more mosques have been burned to the ground, and Muslims have perished in the tens of thousands."

"May they go on killing each other 'til kingdom come, and leave us alone! What have we done to them?"

"It's not a matter of guilt or innocence. It's about the state, don't you see? Minorities can only be protected if there is a strong state. We have neither parties nor militias—or much else to show for ourselves."

Maha was obdurate. Or maybe she just didn't want to abandon the argument on my terms.

"It's not as if it's just here, in Iraq. Look at Egypt. There's a strong state there—and they're still killing Christians and burning down churches! They're going to keep at it until we all leave, just like they did with the Jews. Why did the Jews leave? Who made them go?"

"My dear, what happened with the Jews is entirely different, and it's complicated. Israel had come into the picture, and the Jews were stripped of their nationality with the collusion of the old regime. After that, it just became one huge tangled mess."

Luay had said nothing until now, but not because he had no feelings about the subject.

"It's not just us, Uncle," he said, breaking his silence. "What about the poor Mandaeans and the Yazidis up north? Look at what happened to them. The Muslims aren't going to leave anyone be."

"It's a religion which was spread by the sword. What do you expect?" Maha chimed in.

"And can you tell me how the Christian faith was spread?" I asked her. "By making nice and whispering sweet nothings into people's ears? If it weren't for that Roman emperor— his name escapes me right now—who converted, Christianity wouldn't have spread at the pace it did. Wasn't it the practice

15

of conquering Christian armies to behead people for no other reason than their refusal to convert? And how about the Crusades and the conquest of the Americas which, with the blessing of the church, involved the slaughter of an estimated twenty million people?"

"Well, I don't know about those details, Uncle. And that was all in the past. Our problems are right now, in the present. The Muslims want to get rid of us, quite simply, so that the country can become theirs alone."

"What do you mean 'theirs'? The country belongs to everybody, and if it's anyone's, it's ours, before anyone else, all the way back to the time of the Chaldeans and from there on down to the Abbasids, the Ottomans, and the creation of the modern nation-state. The evidence is there, in all of our museums. We've been here from the very beginning. If it isn't our country, I'd like to know whose it is!"

She sighed, and sounded pained as she answered. "I guess that's where we'll end up, in museums. It may have been our country once, Uncle, a long time ago, in the past. But that's all over. Today, we are all infidels and second-class citizens."

"Infidels, shminfidels! As soon as things settle down, life will be good again. It's just a matter of time. Things are far better now than they were three or four years ago."

"How so, Uncle? What is it that's going to be better after all the killing, the slaughter, and displacement?"

"Maha, my dear, many countries and peoples have gone through far worse, and then things have settled down. That's the cycle of history."

"Please, Uncle, what are you saying? Go outside and see how they're treating people in the streets, and at their jobs, and then come and tell me that it'll all go back to normal. It won't!"

She was red-hot with anger and waved her right hand in the air for emphasis, and although her husband placed his left hand on her arm to get her to tone it down, she carried right on.

"I'd like to know when you think our situation was perfectly stable. When was it that there was no discrimination or racism?"

"With all due respect, dear you're still very young. What's going on now is out of the ordinary. In the old days . . . ."

"Uncle, I know nothing about the old days! Nor do I want to know. All I want is to live with dignity and be treated like a human being!"

"Yes, that is your right. But history . . . ."

She interrupted me again. "What history, for God's sake! You're just living in the past, Uncle!"

6

She was still in bed and hadn't got up yet to get ready for school. I remembered how it was the Gulf War in 1991 that had brought us together, Maha and me. And now, after another war, or rather the devastation and calamities resulting from it, she and her husband had ended up living under the same roof with me. I would never have imagined such a thing. But, honestly, could anyone have ever imagined any of the things that have occurred in recent decades?

During the bombing of Baghdad in 1991, I had wanted to stay in the house, but Hinna was so terrified by the sound of the bombs that she insisted we should go to the shelter where we had relatives. The air force command base was close to where we lived and as she kept repeating to people afterward, the shelling was "right over our heads." When we had argued about going to the shelter, I'd said to her, "If we are meant to die, does it make any difference where we are?"

"In that case," she replied, "let's go and die with our family, then. Surely, that's better than dying alone?"

"What do you think this is? A party?" I told her. "I want to die in my own home."

It wasn't a proper bomb shelter but the basement of the Amira supermarket, which belonged to a relative in the district of Karrada Kharij. Still, it was large enough to accommodate the owner's relatives as well as a few other families who lived close by and had decided to stay put. Many people had left the capital for the provinces a day or two earlier to escape the bombing that had just begun.

The first time I'd met Maha as a little girl, she was sobbing, just as she had been last night, and I had been quite upset by the sight of the fat tears streaming down her face. I'd seen her before that of course, at various family gatherings, but my first clear memory of her was that gloomy night in the shelter when she sobbed in her mother's lap as American jet fighters pounded Baghdad so hard that the earth shook. Other than her mother, Nawal, I'd been the only person who'd been able calm her.

At one point, Nawal got up and start walking around, cradling Maha in her arms, and trying to lull her to sleep. She approached the doorway by the stairs where I stood holding the small transistor radio that went with me everywhere. Even though all they had been saying for the previous forty-eight hours was, "Allied forces continue their aerial bombardment of targets inside Iraq and Kuwait," I felt the need to listen to the news continuously and I couldn't get a signal inside the basement shelter, so I stood in the stairway near the exit, ducking back in whenever the shelling became too intense.

When I saw Maha with her face buried in her mother's chest, Nawal had remarked, "The poor child, she's frightened to death!" but then she turned to her daughter and said, "Look, who's here! It's Uncle Youssef! Let's say hello to him!" Her green eyes brimming with tears, Maha had looked up at me, as if she hadn't heard a thing her mother had said.

"Hey, what's going on? Why all this crying?" I asked.

She pointed her little hand at the ceiling and said, "That."

Chucking her cheek gently, I asked, "That? What's that?"

"Boom, boom, boom," she answered, her eyes glistening, and then put her thumb back in her mouth.

"No, no," I told her, "It's not 'boom, boom.' It's just raining! It's raining really, really hard. Don't worry, it'll be over soon. All gone!"

Her eyes grew wide as if she were thinking over what I had just said. Then she looked to her mother for confirmation and Nawal reassured her. "It's just the rain, darling. Nothing but rain."

Although fear lingered in her eyes, soon Maha was repeating the words "Rain, rain," after her mother. All through the remaining days we spent in the shelter, she would chant, "Lain, lain!" every time the shelling intensified—as if the four letters were an umbrella that would shield her from the manmade cloudbursts that poured down on Baghdad and other Iraqi cities for weeks on end.

Hinna had brought bags of klaicha, sambusak, and cheese fatayer for us to eat in the shelter. I also stocked up on chocolate whenever the store opened for a few hours in between waves of bombing. Following the invasion of Kuwait, we suddenly got British chocolate bars such as Cadbury's and Flake, which I hadn't seen in years. On the wrapper of a particularly good one, with hazelnuts and raisins, it said "Specially imported to Kuwait," and I realized that it was looted merchandise. The same thing happened two months later when I bought a box of cheese, which said, "Danish aid to the Iraqi people."

The Americans' so-called 'surgical strikes' were nothing of the kind. Contrary to what they claimed on the news, the strikes were 'aami shami' as Hinna said—pell-mell, indiscriminate, and random. They mistakenly hit the nearby Ilwiya post office three times, destroying several buildings before hitting their target. I didn't understand the connection between the Ilwiya post office and their campaign to liberate Kuwait. One of the men in the shelter, who smoked almost nonstop just outside the door, had an answer to everything and informed me it was to cut off communication with the army in Kuwait. I found him annoying and wasn't convinced—it seemed ridiculous that the Iraqi army was communicating with troops in Kuwait from this post office.

The day after the Ilwiya post office was hit, I decided to venture out and see for myself. As I approached the side streets, I saw hundreds of pieces of paper strewn on the ground and hanging off palm trees everywhere. I stopped to take a look and saw that they were telephone bills and other mundane official paperwork.

A week into our sojourn at the shelter, there wasn't a drop of water left in the tanks on the roof of the building or in the sole toilet that everyone who didn't have a house nearby was using. It grew awkward and uncomfortable, and Hinna finally agreed that it was time to go home. An anti-aircraft gun position had been set up on the roof of the building next door, and it made such an ear-splitting and terrifying noise that there was practically no difference between being home and being at the shelter.

When we got to the house, we had to clean out the fridge and the freezer and throw away the food that had spoiled after the power was cut off at the start of the bombing. Because it was Lent and we couldn't eat meat, Hinna wanted to throw out meat from the freezer that was still good, but I told her we should use it.

"Haram," I said, "don't throw it away. Food is short, everything is closed."

As we argued over what to do, Heaven intervened and our parish priest dropped by for a visit. He was doing the rounds of the neighborhood to check on his parishioners. When Hinna asked him about the meat, he told her that the church had issued a directive postponing Lent due to the state of emergency.

"Excellent, Father! The Good Lord sent you our way!" I exclaimed.

The first few days, the bombing went on nonstop, but it soon settled into a regular pattern. The 'American fireworks,' as Hinna called the air raids that would start in the evening and go on until daybreak.

"What was with them last night? Boom, boom, boom, boom . . . . Isn't it enough already? Haven't they had their fill yet?" she'd ask, every morning.

In those days, Amer, my sister Salima's son, would come over on his bike from their house in al-Amin. Like everything else, gas was in short supply and the phones didn't work, so bicycles were suddenly a prime means of transportation. Salima sent him over to check on us and he relayed her suggestion that we move in with them. Their house was safer since it wasn't located right by the air force command. Naturally, I objected.

"Thanks, dear boy, but your house is no better. The Rashid barracks are right behind your place so it's six of one and half a dozen of another."

Although Hinna tried to convince me, I wouldn't budge. I told her she was free to go if she wished and I offered to drive her there, despite needing to save what gas I had in the tank in case of an emergency. She hemmed and hawed but stayed put because she couldn't bring herself to leave me alone in the house.

We only had water every three days, and we'd fill as many bottles and plastic pitchers as we could. We also filled the tubs in both ground floor bathrooms, and used that water to flush the toilets. To bathe, we'd heat a big cauldron over palm-tree kindling that I would light in the fireplace in the reception lounge.

"They've turned the clocks back a hundred years," Hinna would exclaim, shaking her head. "In the old days, the fireplace was for sitting around and roasting chestnuts."

Following the cease-fire, the regime's slogans and vocabulary changed. No longer were euphemisms like "returning the branch to the tree" and "the mother of all battles" being used; instead, we heard more mundane phrases such as, "the events of August 2" and, "the allied attack." One day, after the northern and southern uprisings had broken out and I had gone out to get a few things we needed, I noticed that the Secret Police car with tinted windows had disappeared from al-Wathiq Square where it had always sat. According to one of the market vendors in the square who was listening to the radio, there was, "fighting everywhere." For three days in a row, Saddam made no speeches and I heard a report on the radio saying he had lost control of most of the provinces.

He regained the upper hand, of course, after slaughtering thousands of people and throwing them into mass graves.

The first time the power was back after that was in April, on the eve of Saddam's birthday. On his special day, he appeared in a white suit and cut into a birthday cake before a group of children singing and dancing as if nothing had happened. Hinna turned to me. "Can you believe that man carrying on like this? After everything we've been through? Has he no shame? People are dying everywhere, the country is devastated, and he's playing at happy birthday like a little kid! What a disgrace."

7

I needed to withdraw money from the bank and planned to visit my friend Saadoun by the same token. I wouldn't let Maha and her husband pay rent, even though they wanted to. It didn't make much difference to my budget or overall situation—my needs were simple and I had saved much of what my siblings and their children sent our way from time to time. I decided not to take the car as I wasn't going far and had promised myself to heed my doctor's recommendation to walk every day in order to help lower my blood pressure. I returned my tea glass to the sink. I took my blood pressure pill with a little water that I gulped straight from a bottle of mineral water in the fridge without bothering to use a glass. I love cold water, whatever the season.

I went into my room, took off my pajamas, and put on gray trousers and a blue shirt, and wore the comfortable sneakers I used for walking. I looked around my room and in the closet for my navy blue overcoat but couldn't find it. Then I remembered it was hanging in the vestibule. I stepped out of my room, closed the door, and stopped at the stairwell. I pricked up my ears. The door to the second floor was closed and it was completely quiet up there. No matter, I would see Maha before church and we would make up. She was sure to apologize and I would do the same; I realized that I wasn't sufficiently sensitive toward her, especially after what had happened to them in al-Dawra. I crossed the living room and grabbed my coat from the coatrack in the vestibule on the way. I put the coat on, picked up my keys from the wooden table under the rack, and unlocked the three deadbolts. The front door slammed shut as a cold wind blew into my face. I went back to the coatrack to get my black scarf and wrapped it around my neck. I noticed that the door from the vestibule leading to the reception lounge was open. I reached over to shut it and as I did so, glanced at the photographs across the room that hung on the wall next to the wooden bar.

I stepped inside the reception lounge that I no longer used since so few visitors came by and most of our relatives had emigrated. I tripped on the edge of the Kashan rug whose colors I loved, but was able to recover my balance without falling. I went around the coffee table in the center of the room and stood before the archipelago of photographs dotted across the wall. I'd picked them out years ago, and had them nicely framed and hung them at regular intervals from one another. Once again, I recalled the previous night's dream.

Family Photographs

1

No one knows the exact date the photo was taken. But Youssef remembers that it was a Friday a few months before the Haraka, Rashid Ali al-Gaylani's coup in 1941. He was eight years old then. The shot was taken at the old family house, which they shared with Uncle Yuhanna and his family. The Armenian photographer had been going door to door trying to convince residents of the Christian quarter to sit for family portraits. Youssef's father had been hesitant to begin with but they all insisted, and after his own brother, Yuhanna, had agreed to it, and was rounding up his wife and children to sit for a photo, Gorgis came around. The photographer had set up in a corner of the courtyard where the light was just right, and he had them drape a large white cloth across the garden wall as a backdrop.

Abu Youssef, as Gorgis was known, sat solemnly at the center of the photo, wearing a traditional damask robe and a yashmagh wrapped around his head in the style of migrants who had recently arrived from the north. Although he had come to Baghdad three decades earlier, he categorically refused to dress like an effendi and adopt western clothes; he ignored the harping about it, which he heard from everyone, and wore the traditional garb to his dying day in 1957. Youssef sat beside him, but like a flitting bird, he couldn't keep still, and Gorgis had wrapped his left arm around his son's shoulder, clasping the boy's hand in his own. After smoothing his moustache one last time, he'd rested his right hand on his right knee just as the photographer instructed them to stop moving and to look straight at the lens. Pulling out a plate from the camera, the photographer began counting down, "Five, four, three, two, one, zero."

Naima, Gorgis's wife, sat next to him on the other side, smiling confidently. The absence of color in the black and white photo in no way diminished the radiance of the wide, dark eyes that had first captivated Gorgis and made him go back to his village to betroth her. After he'd spent years working in river transport with his cousins, plying the waters between Muhammara and Baghdad, she had assumed that he'd forgotten the village and its inhabitants. Some of the villagers had warned her parents against Gorgis: they considered him cursed because his first wife and her two children had died in a drowning accident. They feared that a similar fate awaited Naima. But her father wasn't in the least swayed by such talk. He was actually happy to marry his daughter to someone he considered to be of good extraction: he and Gorgis's father owned adjoining plots of land in Talkayf where they had farmed barley together their entire lives.

Naima looks happy in the photo; Amal, the last of their brood, was already quite active in her belly, as if she were trying to muscle her way into the picture or play with Salima, the two-year-old seated in her mother's lap. Gorgis had insisted on the name Salima in tribute to Iraq's most famous singer of the time, Salima Murad Pasha. Naima had wanted to bear Gorgis more children to make up for the two that he'd lost in the accident near Muhammara, even though he never talked about it. But two years later, Naima's heart stopped beating after dinner one day. She passed away, leaving a heavy burden to Hinna, her eldest daughter, who, in the family portrait, is sitting beside her and holding onto her mother's right arm. Hinna had to leave school at fifteen to devote herself to doing the cooking and bringing up her siblings, while also working as a seamstress to help keep the family afloat. This went on for five long years, until her brothers finished school and were able to start pulling their weight. The greater sacrifice, from her point of view, was giving up the dream of becoming a nun and devoting her life to God. She never married and instead of being the white-robed virginal bride of Christ she had always dreamed of becoming, she gave up her life for the sake of her siblings.

Habiba, who was three years younger but taller than Hinna, stood right behind her, resting her right hand on her older sister's shoulder, as though to thank her in advance for all that she would do. At the time, she had no idea that she would be part of one of the first generations of nurses to graduate in Iraq or that she would be sent to Sulaymaniya in Iraqi Kurdistan. Gorgis and his daughters would end up moving to the faraway city in order to be by her side during her three-year stint there, while the five boys remained with their uncle in Baghdad. Habiba's salary had been sufficient to support them all, and after a few years she was even able to relieve her father from years of hard work, allowing him to stay home after the accident that led to his retirement.

The photographer had asked Ghazi, Jamil, Elias, and Mikhail, whose ages ranged between four and seven, to sit on the ground at their parents' feet. This was the one and only photograph of the entire family together. Over the years, they scattered, moving to other parts of the country or to other countries where they appeared in other photographs, either alone or in clusters, but never again as a complete group.

2

Ten-year-old Youssef is wearing a white shirt, and a piece of white ribbon tied around his right wrist makes it look as if a large butterfly has landed on him. Encased in soft white gloves, his hands are joined together in prayer and a rosary with a crucifix on the end of it hangs between his index and third fingers—even though he wasn't really praying. His black hair is carefully combed and it looks as if he is trying to stifle a smile. He had been the object of everyone's attention that morning, and all eyes had been on him. He had just completed his First Communion at the nearby Church of Our Mother of Sorrows in the predominantly Christian quarter. Afterward, his father had taken him straight to the studio for a photo to commemorate the day when Jesus had entered his heart. From then on, he was expected to be observant like his elders, to pray every night before going to sleep, to accompany his parents to church every Sunday, and to take confession, and take Holy Communion. The photograph, which was an upper-body portrait, didn't show his white pants or the shoes and new socks that his father had bought him for the occasion. That morning, at Our Mother of Sorrows, he had knelt down in front of a statue of Jesus on the cross and repeated the chants, which they had all learned by heart in the previous weeks. He could still recall some of the verses.

> Holy God, almighty and eternal, have mercy on us. Glory be to the Father, to the Son, and to the Holy Spirit, forever and ever, amen and amen. To You, Lord of all creation, we give thanks. To you, Jesus Christ, our praise.

He had listened to the sermon by the patriarch who had officiated at the ceremony and had placed the host in his mouth with his own hand. He could still taste the body of Christ moistened with his blood, which is how the patriarch described the wafer dipped in wine. He had remembered to let the wafer melt in his mouth and not to bite down on it because it was the friable body of Christ. At the ceremony now in the studio, he knelt before the camera, and instead of the patriarch, there was an Armenian photographer officiating, asking him in broken Arabic to look straight at the camera lens without moving. Youssef was puzzled because the man had addressed him as a girl, but when he saw the smile on his father's face, he understood that this was a peculiarity of the photographer's speech.

They went home afterward, joining his mother and siblings who had gone back to the house ahead of them. His mother had prepared a celebratory breakfast that she'd laid out on a big table in the courtyard where both their family and his uncle's family were assembled. Taking advantage of all the commotion, Youssef stuffed himself with delicious kahi with gaymar, which his uncle had brought, and ate as many bread wraps as he could. He loved the paper-thin bread rolled around a filling of cheese and homemade jam which his mother made, and Hinna kept on rolling them because she couldn't deny him anything that day. The next day, he was laid up in bed. All that food, followed by running around and playing with his siblings and cousins had done him in, and given him an upset stomach. His mother had chided him, saying he had no self-control, "Ay ma eeth brayshukh? Satana?"

Jesus may have entered his heart, she said, but the devil was still in his head! Their mother, who was a relatively recent arrival from the village, only spoke to them and their father in Chaldean. They all understood her but they answered her in Arabic.

3

The graduating class of 1950 stood in front of the main building of Baghdad College, right under the large sign with the school's name emblazoned on it, in both English and Arabic, along with a short reference to the Jesuits who had founded the school and taught there. Seven students stood in the back row against the school's imposing door. One step down, another eight formed the middle row. Father O'Casey, who was from Boston, stood in the center of the first row flanked by three students on either side. Second from the right in the back row was Youssef, whose face and upper chest alone were visible. Standing between Nasim Hizkayl and Salem Hussein, his long arms were spread like wings across his friends' shoulders, drawing them closer. It was not surprising that the three

29

of them lined up next to each other: they always sat together in class and spent recess together in the quad—so much so, that Father O'Casey called them the 'pack of wolves.'

"No, Father," Youssef had told him, "we're a harmless flock of birds."

Soon after graduation, the flock dispersed, however. Salem went to medical school and his father, who was a prominent businessman, interceded on Youssef's behalf and got him his first job as a legal translator with the Iraqi Date Palm Authority. If it weren't for the scholarships the school offered to outstanding students from modest families, Youssef would never have attended Baghdad College. Nasim, for his part, went to work for the import-export firm called Andrew Weir. Although their lives got busy, the three of them would meet up from time to time, and they never imagined that the flock would lose one of its members.

Just weeks before the photograph was taken, the government passed the 1950 emigration law stripping Iraqi Jews of their citizenship. Yet Nasim appeared unworried when Youssef and Salem questioned him about the rumors of a Jewish exodus; his father gave the idea no credence, Nasim said. He would repeat his father's words that it was nothing but a passing cloud, and they were not leaving Iraq. The violence of the Farhud had been truly scary when it happened years before, but it was over, and things had settled down. Although there were still occasional attacks, the situation was bound to improve.

About a year after the photograph was taken, the three of them were strolling along the banks of the Tigris. Nasim was quiet that day, he seemed really preoccupied and his handsome features were drawn. His eyes, indeed his entire face, were bathed in gloom. Only after Salem had pestered him about looking so miserable did Nasim reveal what weighed on his heart.

"This may be the last time we ever see each other," he said.

"Why? Where are you going?" a bewildered Youssef asked naively.

"My father has registered our names under the emigration law. We're going to Israel."

A heavy silence descended on them. There'd been five attacks on Jewish properties and other places that were frequented by Jews, and the Masuda Shimtov Synagogue had been firebombed. Although it later transpired that the perpetrators had been Zionist militants, the attacks succeeded in frightening Iraq's Jewish community. Nasim said his father was no longer allowed to do business, his assets had been frozen, and his property confiscated. That was why the family had decided to join the rest of the community and register for emigration.

Nothing was audible but the sound of their footsteps and the rustle of the palm trees, whose branches swayed in the breeze that had stirred up as if to bid Nasim goodbye. When Youssef asked about his departure date, Nasim said he wasn't sure when they would be leaving.

"Probably in a couple of days," he ventured.

Youssef was having a hard time understanding how it had all come to this. "How long will you be gone?" he asked. It was a question without an answer. With a brash optimism, bordering on naïveté, Salem tried to dispel the sadness that had taken hold of them, "Don't worry, you'll only be gone a few months. As soon as the question of Palestine is settled, you'll be back."

Nasim was tearful as they said goodbye in front of his house in Battawiyin. They hugged him fiercely and he told them he'd write from there, but no letters ever arrived. Salem couldn't believe that he would never see Nasim again. From time to time in the months that followed, he'd insist on walking down the street where their friend had lived, but the house always looked abandoned. Over the years, Nasim was fondly remembered whenever Youssef and Salem reminisced about their youth.

4

Wearing a dark suit and tie, Youssef is sitting at a desk littered with papers and files. In the early weeks, his job responsibilities were limited to translating foreign correspondence from English into Arabic and writing letters pertaining to contracts, offers, and bids or translating them into English. When work was slow and he was bored, Youssef would browse through the books in the small government agency's library. Most were about agriculture and commerce and one entitled *Sacred Tree: The Date Palm in Semitic Civilizations*, by British Orientalist Sir Roger Kingsley, piqued his interest. Youssef kept a notebook where he wrote down the more difficult words he came across which he needed to look up in the dictionary. The idea soon formed in his mind to translate the book—the writing was fluid and the book was a mine of historical information. He started on the project, translating a little every day or whenever he had a chance to work on it.

He was fascinated by the introduction, which recounted the history of the date palm and its almost sacred role in Mesopotamia. There was ample evidence for this in the sculptures and bas-reliefs of sanctuaries in Babylon and Assur, on temple walls and city gateways, as well as on ceremonial thrones and crowns. Used medicinally, dates were also used to produce the 'elixir of life.' Cutting down a date palm tree was punishable by a fine under the Code of Hammurabi. Another section of the code warned date palm farmers against neglecting their orchards and enjoined them to be vigilant about pruning and pollination. Palm tree fronds symbolized both victory and good fortune, and were carried as such by kings. An entire chapter devoted to the role of the date palm in Islam pointed out its centrality in the Islamic tradition, from the Quranic sura named after Mary in which she shakes the date palm until she is blessed with its fertile fruit, to the descriptions of Paradise where dates, pomegranates, and other fruits await believers. The author also referenced a saying attributed to the Prophet Muhammad according to which, "in a house without dates, the inhabitants go hungry."

Over time, the date palm also became sacred to Youssef as he became indebted to it, and to all its siblings, for his livelihood. Even though he did not labor with his own hands to grow and care for the tree, he spent more than half his life working at the Iraqi Date Palm Authority.

5

Wearing a white summer shirt, gray trousers, and sunglasses, Youssef is standing beside a date palm, his left hand buried in his trouser pocket, and his right resting on the trunk of the towering tree. Its fronds shade him from the blazing sun casting the tree's shadow across a long line of others. Youssef appears in the prime of youth and in good health. The photo was taken by a man who appears in the next picture on the wall standing beside Youssef. His name was Jasim Abul-Shawk, but everyone knew him as Abul-Nakhl, Mr. Date Palm, because his life was dedicated to the study of Iraqi date palms; he not only wanted to know everything there was to know about them but he was also determined to boost their yields.

Jasim was from Abul-Khasib and his father, who was a wealthy businessman, had sent him to the American University of Beirut. From there, he went on to Berkeley in the U.S., one of a group of students sponsored to study horticulture abroad by the Department of Religious Endowments in the 1930s. Jasim obtained both his undergraduate and master's degrees with distinction and wrote his thesis on the pests and diseases common to date palms. Back in Iraq, he joined the Ministry of Agriculture where he quickly rose through the ranks. He also lectured at Baghdad University's School of Agriculture and founded a model farm in Zaafaraniya where he carried out research on every species of date palm in the country.

They had met when Youssef had visited Zaafaraniya on an assignment to write a report about the model farm. Their acquaintance developed further after Youssef got permission from his then boss to attend Jasim's lectures weekly so as to deepen his knowledge of the subject. Youssef asked a lot of questions, both during and after the lectures, and his enthusiasm and seriousness impressed Jasim. It was Youssef's good fortune that Jasim was appointed to head the Authority's board of directors two years later. Jasim was so taken by Youssef's dedication that he began to nominate him to join commercial delegations traveling abroad to promote Iraqi dates and also backed his promotion within the Authority. A deep bond developed between the two of them, and every time Youssef told his friend that he was truly Abul-Nakhl, Mr. Date Palm, Jasim responded by saying, "And you are the Master of the Palm Fronds, Ibn al-Nakhl." Youssef's heart was stricken when Abul-Nakhl resigned in 1964 as a result of some intrigue on the part of Tahir Yahya, the prime minister at the time. After that, Abul-Nakhl devoted himself to his family's orchard in Abul-Khasib and to completing a voluminous tome on the date palm tree.

"Be careful . . . those guys are going to ruin it all," he told Youssef that day.

When they hugged goodbye, Jasim said he'd never worked with anyone better and he assured Youssef that if it weren't for the fact that he didn't have a degree, he could easily have risen to head the Ministry of Agriculture or, at the very least, become deputy minister. Those who succeeded Jasim had neither his field experience nor the required academic credentials. Invariably political appointees, they were entirely dependent on Youssef, the senior-most official at the Authority who was by now not only knowledgeable but exceptionally experienced. Youssef's independence protected him whenever the winds of change began to blow. A succession of rulers appeared in the picture frame above his desk, from the monarch to Abdel-Karim Qasim, and from Abdel-Salam Arif to Abdel-Rahman Arif, and on down to Ahmed Hassan al-Bakr, during whose regime Youssef became the director-general of the agency as a result of his longevity in service. Saddam Hussein came along after that and his picture was still up on the wall when Youssef retired many years later.

Youssef didn't remember when exactly his love affair with the date palm began, but his feelings gradually grew stronger as a result of his job and all the reading he did about the amazing plant when he was just starting out. He did remember very clearly jumping up in the air as a little boy, his arm reaching for the bunch of dates that his father regularly bought at the market and hung outside. "I want one, I want one," he would shout, and Hinna would come out and pick the almost-ripe dates for him. At the old house in the Christian quarter, they didn't have a courtyard, and when they moved to Battawiyin, there was only one solitary date palm in the small courtyard there. But in the new house, which is old now—and where Youssef still lives—the garden was spacious enough for three palm saplings. Although one of them died, the remaining ones grew to be taller than the house.

Youssef didn't know that racemes like those he struggled to reach would one day become his livelihood, and that they would nurture him for the rest of his life. Nor could he have guessed that the date palm, which was so sacred to the ancients as a source of life and sustenance, would attain a similarly elevated standing in his eyes one day. There was nothing strange about it, he felt. Anyone who chose to delve into its history and uncover its riches could not help but become enamored of the date palm.

6

It was the Nowruz festival, and even though the colors didn't translate into the monochrome of black and white, Youssef's sisters, Amal and Salima, were wearing traditional, brightly colored, embroidered Kurdish dresses. They were standing in front of a house whose imposing wooden door was clearly visible; a year apart, the two girls were eleven and twelve. The stone house was in Sulaymaniya, the city they lived in for four years after Habiba got her first posting following graduation from nursing school. Gorgis had moved there because in the

1950s it was unthinkable that Habiba might live by herself in a strange and faraway city. He'd taken Salima and Amal with him and the two girls had struggled at the beginning because of the language barrier. Everyone in Sulaymaniya spoke Kurdish, and they would only be able to communicate with their schoolmates after they too had learned to speak it. Back in Baghdad, they continued to use it as their secret language; even though their father scolded them for it, they would resort to Kurdish whenever they didn't want others to know what they were saying.

7

Youssef loved to brag about his affair with Sophia Loren. It went way back and continued even after she married Carlo Ponti, he'd say. On hearing this, people would simply burst out laughing. Undeterred, he would tell his interlocutors that it wasn't just a pipe dream, and that although he was one among millions of her admirers, he and Sophia corresponded regularly and met once every few years. Whenever he traveled with an official delegation from the Date Authority to Europe, she would come to visit him in the city where they were staying. He would then urge his disbelieving audience to see for themselves. He'd walk them to the lounge and show them a photograph taken in 1972 where the two of them appear side by side as he leans over to kiss her. The sight of this photo would elicit responses ranging from incredulity to amazement and admiration, followed by a babble of questions and pleas for more details and other pictures of him and his Italian sweetheart. Youssef would provide whatever answer he fancied and then he'd own up: the photograph had been taken at Madame Tussauds, the London wax museum, and the stiff and frozen likeness of Sophia he was about to kiss was the polar opposite of the hot-blooded movie bombshell. What's more, his attempted kiss had earned him a rebuke from one of the guards because he had disobeyed the prominently posted signs asking visitors to refrain from touching the wax figures.

8

A year younger than Youssef, Ghazi was the second of the boys. He'd always been stockier than his siblings, even when he was young. The photo was taken in 1959 when Ghazi and his wife, Samira, were in their mid-twenties. He's dressed in a suit and tie, while the lovely Samira sports a low-cut sleeveless dress that shows off her cleavage. They're sitting at a table strewn with plates, glasses, and bottles, and behind them one can see men and women dancing in the hall of IPC's club in Kirkuk. Ghazi is frowning for no reason, as always, but Samira is smiling for the camera.

Ghazi went to work for IPC—the Iraq Petroleum Company—in Kirkuk and remained there until 1961 when he returned to Baghdad and got a job with Rabco, a paint manufacturing company. There was always a certain distance between Ghazi and the rest of them, and even after he and Samira returned from Kirkuk, he only came by the old family house on holidays, and did only the bare minimum to maintain his connection to them. Hinna blamed it on Samira. She accused her of spiriting him away to her people when they came back to live in Baghdad and of convincing him to leave for the U.S. after three of her brothers emigrated there. In 1979, they emigrated and settled in Michigan, where Ghazi bought a store that he co-owned for many years, before eventually retiring to San Diego, California.

Youssef had always known Ghazi to be distant; ever since childhood, he'd been the least warm of all the siblings. After he left Iraq, they would go long periods without any news. Ghazi never offered to help out like Salima and Amal did, during the 1990s, without Youssef even asking. Ghazi always ended a conversation with the formulaic, "You need anything?" to which Youssef invariably responded with, "No, hamdullilah, everything's fine."

Hinna and Youssef were both surprised in 2000 when they got a call from one of Ghazi's grandchildren who was in

Baghdad with a group of activists delivering medical supplies to Iraqi hospitals and, thus, symbolically breaking the embargo. Although he was just twenty years old, Basil, who was born and raised in the U.S., spoke almost fluent Arabic. He struggled with rolling his *r*'s and pronouncing his *l*'s properly, but his Arabic warranted a "Paha!" from Hinna—an exclamation reserved for exceptional achievements or things that truly impressed her. Basil was studying political science at UCLA and he had developed an interest in Iraqi and Middle Eastern history. He had become politicized in college and had joined Los Angeles area activists opposed to the sanctions regime, volunteering to travel with a delegation on a visit to area hospitals, as well as the Amiriya shelter and the National Museum in Baghdad. Youssef and Hinna had urged him to stay with them but Basil felt he should stay at the hotel with the rest of the group. He made sure to visit more than once, however, and Hinna cooked kubbah hamudh and biryani for him. He spent his last night in Baghdad with them following the small party they gave for their remaining relatives in Baghdad to come and meet the visiting émigré.

9

Elias, the third brother, is in his early thirties. His hair is jet black, his radiant face lit by a broad smile, and he's wearing an elegant black suit. Shakeh, his Armenian wife, is in her white wedding dress and her long gloves come all the way up above her elbows. They're holding hands and smiling. They met as a result of Elias's political activities, and Shakeh was the sister of his comrade, Mano. Youssef wasn't surprised when Elias got involved in politics and became a Communist. He'd always liked a good argument, even as a small child. They used to call him 'Mr. No' and 'Hellion' because he was forever criticizing and opposing everything.

He was the only son who went to university, where he studied law, but was repeatedly jailed for his politics. In spite of everything he went through, Elias remained a bon vivant, more so than the rest of them. There wasn't a wedding where he wasn't dancing or singing, and when no one else could move anymore, he just kept going, a glass of araq always at hand. After years in jail, he eventually gave up politics, but they were always watching and following him around. The last time he was jailed he had been working as legal counsel for a Yugoslav construction firm that had a number of projects in the country during the 1980s. The company director had asked him to deliver an envelope to one of the employees, and after he did, a member of the local staff reported him for "accepting bribes from foreigners." The accusation cost him another three years in jail. Prison didn't break him, but it wore him down. He remained physically fit but he tired of life, especially during the long years of sanctions. Then he began losing his memory. He'd forget the simplest things and would sometimes get lost when out on his regular evening walk. At her insistence, his wife began accompanying him, but one day in 1999, he slipped out of the house in his pajamas while she was still asleep and he never came back. They found him at the coroner's office a week later. His body had been picked up in a small alley off Rashid Street. When the residents of the area were questioned, they said he'd been roaming the neighborhood for several days and they couldn't make head or tail of what he wanted or was after, and he had no ID or wallet on him. Someone had eventually found him lying against a wall; he had died of thirst and hunger.

During the embargo and after years of deprivation, people changed: everybody was overwhelmed by their own problems and no one had reached out to him or tried to help. Why Elias had wandered to that particular neighborhood, nobody in the family could fathom.

On the third day of mourning, one of Elias's friends came to offer his condolences, and as he sipped on his coffee, the conversation turned to the circumstances of Elias's death.

"Good gracious," the friend exclaimed, "we used to meet in a house over there during our days underground!"

Elias's Alzheimer's, or whatever dementia afflicted him, had erased everything except for that old party haunt. His wife found no solace in the story, and she reiterated her view that politics had robbed her of everything: first, her brother who'd been executed in 1979, and then her husband, whose mind had been destroyed.

10

Youssef is seated at the head of a large table laden with food. He is grinning broadly and holding up a very full glass of araq, which he is about to clink with his brother Jamil, seated to his right. Samia, Jamil's Lebanese wife, is sitting next to her husband and remains, in her forties, as attractive as ever. Looking straight into the camera and smiling, she too holds up her glass in a toast. Seated to Youssef's left is Hinna, the only adult whose glass isn't filled with araq. It contains, instead, a soft drink that the waiter had brought out after Jamil had exclaimed in his best Lebanese accent, "She's not a drunk like the rest of us! Get her a soft drink. She and the little one drink soda!"

To ensure he would be in the picture Fadi, the five-year-old boy sitting next to Hinna, is sticking his head out. Danny, two years younger, isn't in the picture because they'd left him at home with his grandmother. The table, heaving with delicious mezze, was at one of the fabled Zahleh "casinos"—outdoor restaurants located along a gurgling watercourse under the shade of leafy trees in the town of Zahleh. Hinna was smiling happily: it was the first time in five years that they'd seen Jamil, and except for a little gray in his hair, he remained largely unchanged. The three weeks whizzed by as if they'd been three days.

In that time, Hinna was able to visit the renowned pilgrimage site of Our Lady of Lebanon in Harissa, and to pray in the church built at the feet of the massive statue of the Virgin Mary situated on the hilltop.

Jamil had started out working for Shakir Ibrahim and Bros., and left for Beirut in 1969 after a close friend of his was charged with being a Freemason. He remained in Lebanon for the rest of his life, and never set foot in Iraq again, not even for a visit. During this particular visit, Hinna admonished Jamil and his wife repeatedly for not coming to see them.

"You want Jamil to come to Baghdad so they can jail him or sentence him to death?" countered Samia. For Hinna, that was just hyperbole.

"Jail! Samia, how you love to exaggerate!" she retorted.

Hinna would always recall the overland journey she and Youssef made in one of those huge buses that set off from Baghdad and arrived the following day in Beirut, after stops in Amman and Damascus. The situation in Lebanon had been tense but it never occurred to any of them that the country would be engulfed by civil war for years on end. They wouldn't see each other again until 2001 when Jamil traveled to Amman from Beirut after Hinna's tearful entreaties on the phone.

"Dear boy," she'd said, "I want to see you one more time before I die."

11

By the time the middle sister, Salima, graduated high school with distinction in 1956, the family's economic fortunes had vastly improved. Youssef's salary, alongside Habiba's from her nursing work and what Ghazi sent from Kirkuk, afforded them a good life. The Jesuits had just opened al-Hikma University in Zaafaraniya, and Youssef encouraged his sister to apply. Salima was overjoyed when he offered to pay for her to attend. She had always dreamed of becoming an engineer and that is what she studied for in the four years she spent at al-Hikma. Everybody was so proud of her and they all went to her graduation in Zaafaraniya, which was attended by the nationalist leader and then-prime minister Abdel-Karim Qasim. Known as the Zaeem, 'the leader,' Qasim personally handed their diplomas to the students graduating with honors. Salima was pro-Qasim, and she was always arguing with

Hinna who favored King Faysal and was heartbroken by the way he and the royal family were killed. Salima insisted that it wasn't Qasim who had issued the order but Abdel-Salam Arif. After Qasim was executed three years later, Hinna forgot her opposition to him and bemoaned the Zaeem's sorry fate.

Salima was wearing a black dress that she had bought for the occasion even though Hinna had said it was, "shorter than necessary." The hem of the dress fell just above the knees, and pulled up further when she sat. But her graduation gown provided the requisite modesty during the ceremony, hiding her knees and covering her breasts. Because of her rather high heels, Salima climbed up the steps to the stage gingerly. Even though she was a little flustered, she smiled as she shook hands with the Zaeem and thanked him for the diploma with high distinction which the dean had given him to hand out. She couldn't believe that he had spoken to her and had congratulated her personally. "Alf mabrouk, binti" he'd said, as the camera lens blinked and captured the moment.

12

Amal, the youngest girl, is wearing a white dress and a matching headscarf tied under her chin. She's looking down at a baby, barely two months old, in her lap. Only twenty at the time, Amal wouldn't marry and have children until after she had graduated university with a degree in management and economics. The baby in the photo is her niece—her sister Habiba wanted her to be the godmother to May, a girl who'd come on the heels of two boys. Amal is standing in front of a small basin filled with water. The bishop's hand is raised in the air, drawing an invisible cross to bless the water in which May is to be baptized, in emulation of Jesus's baptism in the Jordan River. To Amal's right is Habiba, in a brocade dress and the same dark-colored headscarf worn by the other women in the congregation. Her hand is extended toward the baby who is howling like a cat before water. Abed, the father, is standing to Habiba's right, with a broad grin on his face and his hands behind his back. This was the first family celebration at which Youssef was able to use the expensive Leica he'd purchased in Bonn on a work trip in 1961. He snapped photos inside the church, as well as in the adjoining courtyard, and in the backyard of the house where they all gathered to celebrate afterward. He took dozens of pictures, which were stored in albums or boxes with hundreds of others, and he'd picked out this particular one to hang in the reception room. Maha's husband, Luay, had repeatedly offered to scan them onto a disk at his office and to upload them to Facebook so that all their scattered relatives could see them, but Youssef just kept putting him off.

13

Mikhail, the youngest of the boys, was the spoiled baby of the family and the apple of his father's eye—perhaps because Gorgis had spent more time with him than with any of the other children. Gorgis had become homebound with back pain after suffering an injury on one of his trips upriver when he had lost his footing and taken a fall. Mikhail—or Mikha as Gorgis liked to call him—was a scoundrel: he was smart and had a razor-sharp wit, and he'd joke and banter with his father until he had him in stitches. Gorgis was enthralled by Mikha's cleverness, and all the questions he asked. He could deny him nothing: whatever took the boy's fancy would have his father reaching into his pocket for the money with which to purchase it. Hinna's warnings that such indulgence would spoil him went unheeded, and when Gorgis died in his sleep, Mikhail was so grief-stricken it took him months to recover. He had graduated from Baghdad College, like Youssef and Jamil, and like Youssef, became a translator. He had gone to work for a British firm in the H-3 zone, not far from the Jordanian border, coming back home every Thursday night to spend the weekend with his family. That particular Thursday, he knew as soon as he got back that something awful had happened. Gorgis wasn't sitting in his usual place—on the sofa in the living room—where he sometimes even slept. Instead, Mikhail beheld the sight of his father's body being washed and readied for the funeral service at Our Mother of Sorrows that would take place the next morning and be followed by burial at Sahat al-Tayaran cemetery.

Later, Mikhail would turn to a life of pleasure and dissipation, showering himself with the indulgence that his father had formerly bestowed on him. He worked for a number of foreign companies and his large salary facilitated his profligacy and he drank and partied to his heart's content. When his siblings remonstrated with him, he pointed out that so long as he contributed to the household's expenses, he was free to do as he pleased with his time. He often came home in the wee hours having forgotten his keys, and would call out Amal's name until she woke up. As the youngest of the girls, Amal was the one closest to him, and she would come down from the roof where they slept in the summers in order to let him in.

In all his pictures, Mikhail is either smoking, drinking, or dancing. The photo on the wall shows a handsome young man in his twenties with short, black hair. He is standing next to a friend, and the two of them are cheering, bottles of beer held aloft as they lean against the hood of the friend's car. In the background is Taq Kisra, the site of an ancient triumphal arch and a favorite picnic stop on road trips. That handsome young man is how Youssef liked to recall his brother. Whenever Hinna pleaded with Mikhail to cut back on his drinking, he responded by reminding her that Jesus's first miracle was the conversion of water into wine at the wedding at Cana in Galilee—a clear sign, he'd say, for "those who have eyes to see."

Mikhail was a gifted linguist: in addition to English, which he'd mastered under the tutelage of Baghdad College's 'fatherhood,' he had also learned German after years of work with Züblin, the German company in charge of building the Samarra Dam. Later, he became a broker for a consortium of Australian firms bidding on Iraqi contracts. Mikhail's cut was one percent, and when the consortium landed a deal to help modernize Iraq's agriculture after two years of negotiations, he and the rest of his family had been assured of a life of luxury for the remainder of their days, as the contract ran into the hundreds of millions of dinars. However, because of a clause holding it liable for losses incurred in the event of a natural disaster, the Iraqi government changed its mind, and the deal fell through an hour before the signing ceremony. Mikhail sank into a deep depression and stayed home for an entire year without work.

Even though he eventually landed a job at the Australian Embassy, thanks to the encouragement and support of friends, and resumed normal life, he never got over the setback. He'd leave the embassy in the Hindiya district after work and make his way to the Ilwiya Club to meet up with his drinking buddies. He'd teeter home drunk at eight or nine in the evening, have a bite of dinner, and go to bed alone. His wife refused to sleep in the same room because she could no longer stand his drunkenness or his snoring. He almost never attended family celebrations or visited relatives. He couldn't get over the bad cards fate had dealt him, or the lost opportunity of a lifetime that had destroyed his dreams and made him a wreck. Doctors' warnings and recommendations were in vain: he would not give up his daily drinking or chain-smoking and would crow that he was still alive despite a doctor's prediction in 1967 that he would die from smoking within a year. "Even the Angel of Death has lost his way with me," he'd joke—but the Grim Reaper claimed his reward soon enough.

14

Dating back to 1990 when the family celebrated Wisam's First Communion, the sole color photo on the wall held within its frame almost all the family tree's limbs and fruits. Wisam was Salima's grandson, May's eldest boy, and as her house in the Baladiyat wasn't large enough to accommodate the many guests attending the occasion, Salima had asked Youssef and Hinna if she could hold the celebration in the courtyard of the old family house. Except for Jamil who was in Lebanon and Ghazi who was in America, all of Gorgis Hanna Baharatli's children, as well as their children and grandchildren, appear in the picture. No other photo after this one would bring them together again. The invasion of Kuwait took place less than a month later, following that there was another war, and after that came a prolonged blockade. Slowly, all the brothers and sisters fell away from the family tree, either swept up on the winds of exile or returning to the earth in the plot that the family had bought at the new Chaldean cemetery on the road to Baaquba—the capital's cemeteries were overflowing with the dead and there wasn't a square foot of land to spare. Mikhail was the first to go. He died of a heart attack on the last day of that year, just a few weeks before the war, and his death ushered in a decade that would witness the dissolution and final dispersal of the family. Habiba was next, and she died within a year and a half after cancer had spread throughout her bones. Heat and dementia killed Elias. After 2003, the remaining siblings and their grandchildren scattered to the four winds, ending up in Sweden, Canada, and even New Zealand.

15

There were more photos, some on top of the television, and others hanging on walls in various parts of the house. And of course hundreds more in albums, envelopes, and plastic bags piled inside the third ground-floor bedroom which had gradually turned into a storage area. In the late 1990s and after the 2003 invasion, every relative leaving the country would sell what could be sold, carry what could be carried, and park a few remaining bags and possessions in the family house in the hope that these could somehow be forwarded to them in the future. But the bags and boxes just piled up, gathering dust and awaiting the return of someone to take them to new homes far from Baghdad.

There was one picture that Youssef kept in a small envelope in the bedroom closet that he hadn't taken out in years. In the past, he had often reviewed the many copies of it that lined the walls of his heart and soul. Although the recesses of his heart had darkened in the autumn of his life, they would light up from time to time as his memory stirred. There were changes in some of the details that he alone could see, but the basic elements remained constant: a smiling woman (she always smiled whenever he looked at her); the shiny brown eyes that were the color of the chocolate he so loved and that echoed the glimmer of her beautiful smile; the long black hair that sometimes hid the earrings which she chose ever so carefully. Sometimes he'd glimpse her laughing, covering her mouth with tapered fingers even though she had pretty teeth that were white and straight. Dalal was her name—it was a good designation, for Dalal was true to the enchantment that her name signified.

When she was hired at the agency in 1971, she turned Youssef's world topsy-turvy. She had come with a master's degree in agriculture from the University of Edinburgh and was appointed to a newly created position responsible for development and planning in the date sector. The government's economic policy had been entirely focused on oil and the petroleum industry until then, and with the country undergoing rapid changes, the date sector had been adversely affected. Date palm orchards suffered neglect as migration from the countryside increased, and other date-producing states entered the international market and competed with what had hitherto been Iraq's undisputed monopoly. One of Dalal's first tasks was to conduct a countrywide study on the state of date production in concert with the regional branches of the agency.

She stole his heart the very first time she set foot inside his office with Abu Shukri, the agency's director, who was making the rounds introducing her. She wore a blue jacket with a white blouse underneath, and a skirt that was a slightly paler shade of blue and skimmed her knees. Black stockings and modest heels completed her outfit. Her elegance was distinctive but understated: barely a whiff of makeup and just a small gold Quran on a fine chain around her neck.

Youssef got up, hand outstretched. A smile spread across her face, lighting up her eyes.

"Mr. Youssef, head of the export department. Miss Dalal, our new hire. Today is her first day with us and it's my pleasure to introduce her to everyone," declared Abu Shukri.

She shook his hand firmly and with confidence, unlike many women he knew whose grip was so limp and lifeless that one regretted shaking hands with them at all. Youssef watched her svelte silhouette as she strode out of his office, and her scent hung in the air even after the director had shut the door. He tried turning his attention back to the papers before him, but that scent was like a raincloud of femininity that had burst above his head and it played havoc with his thoughts. He put his palm to his nostrils and inhaled the fragrance which, from now on, he would smell every single morning as he passed her office, which was fortunately on the same floor as his.

At the time, Youssef was in his mid-forties, unmarried, and without children. He'd had plenty of opportunity to sow his wild oats and had frequented nightclubs. There'd been a sad romance with his cousin, Najat, when he was in his twenties. Very much in love, Youssef had wanted to marry Najat, and the two families had agreed that she would be his if her younger sister, Hayat, was betrothed to his brother Ghazi. Hayat, however, didn't have a quarter of Najat's charms and Ghazi was in love with another woman whom he was determined to wed. The ensuing rift between the two families persisted until Gorgis's death and only then did it end, when Najat's father joined the rest of the family for the requisite condolence period. By that time, Najat was married to another man and had two children. For years afterward, there were knowing glances between them but she and Youssef never exceeded the rules of propriety, their exchanges remaining entirely formal, in keeping with social convention. As far as Youssef was concerned, Najat was the love of his life and he would never again love another woman like that, or consider marriage and having children. He liked being unattached, he enjoyed his unencumbered life, and had yet to meet a woman who could persuade him to change his mind.

Until Dalal came along and upset all his calculations. At first, he tried to reason with himself and suppress his feelings. She was more than twenty years his junior and she surely couldn't find him attractive. He was old enough to be her father. Furthermore, she was a Muslim and he was a Christian, which constituted an impossible social barrier. Not only that, but she had a master's degree while he, despite his eminent position, had not gone to university—another thing that made them incompatible in the eyes of society. He was vulnerable and these rationalizations were to protect him, a defense against disappointment he could well do without. Still, his armor soon fell away and Youssef found himself defenseless, with his heart fluttering like a feather every time she passed him, whether in the flesh or in his mind's eye.

During her first week on the job, she came into his office to ask him a question. Seeing the Arabian jasmine he kept on his desk, she expressed delight with the beautiful and fragrant plant. It was from his garden, he told her proudly. The following morning, he took his courage in both hands and offered her a jasmine flower. She thanked him, blushing.

Even though he had not declared himself, he began to wonder whether her glances might reciprocate his feelings, but he quickly banished the thought and told himself that he was deluded. Driving home after work one day, he spotted her not far from the office. It was raining and she was trying to shield her hair with a newspaper as she walked. He hesitated for an instant but then stopped, rolled down the window, and called out to her, offering to drive her home. She thanked him and declined the offer politely, saying she wouldn't want to put him out. He insisted. "And you'd rather put yourself out by walking in the rain?" he said, leaning across to open the passenger door.

She accepted his offer and got in beside him. The downpour had been a complete surprise—it was warm and no one had been expecting rain. Youssef had never felt as happy about the rain as he did on that occasion. The rain was Youssef's good fortune that day: it had soaked Dalal's hair and seeped through her blouse so that it clung fetchingly to her pear-shaped breasts. He also got a glimpse of her knees as she settled into the seat. She tugged at her skirt to cover them and eventually just placed her handbag over them. The rain had softened the ground and connected together the myriad of rivulets that ran between them.

He made conversation and asked her general questions about her studies and the two years she had spent in Britain. She was the only girl in her family and had an older brother who had become a physician. Their father taught in the Engineering Department at Baghdad University and had obtained his doctorate in the U.S. She too wanted to know his story, and asked him about his job and other, slightly more personal questions. The time flew by and she apologized as she requested that he let her off a few streets before they reached her house in Muhandiseen, so as to avert gossip on the part of the neighbors. He assured her that he understood, saying, "We're still quite conservative, as a society, aren't we?"

He looked for every opportunity to offer her a ride home and one day when she said she was hungry, he suggested they go and get something to eat together. She agreed. He relished the time they spent talking after he had stopped the car to let her off at the usual place. He thought carefully before taking the next step that would transform their relationship into a more intimate one, because he was afraid of scaring her off. She had once confided in him how much she missed her outings along the river that ran through the little town close to her university in Britain; he suggested that they could do the same thing in Baghdad and she agreed. He would take her to Masbah Park and to the al-Fahama area, and after she'd bought herself a small car with her father's help, they began meeting in the evenings. She would tell her parents that she was going to visit one of her girlfriends after work. The first time he took her hand as they sat in the car, she didn't object and, on the contrary, squeezed his hand tightly in hers. This progressed to passionate kisses and caresses after they'd park in one of the few places where lovers went (these could be counted on the fingers of one hand) either in al-Fahama or at the end of Abu Nuwas Street on the Jadiriya side. Bringing her home was out of the question, with Hinna in most of the day, except for her trips to the market after church.

Youssef was so smitten with Dalal that he was ready to risk everything to be with her. He was prepared to convert to Islam if necessary—signing a piece of paper or mumbling a few words were no big deal, as far as he was concerned. After he broached the subject of marriage, Dalal approached her father. Not only was he displeased right away, but after getting the answers to two questions, he became adamantly opposed to the idea. Youssef was not in the least suitable as a husband, he told her: even if he converted to Islam, he remained much older than she was and he didn't have a degree. He found her gullibility surprising, he said.

Clearly, her father's education in the United States had done nothing to soften his inflexible thinking. For his part, Youssef didn't broach it with Hinna—he already knew what she thought of marriage to non-Christians from what she said about people who, "got into trouble and did the vile deed." Her answer would be a flat no. And even if marrying Dalal didn't remain a mere fantasy and became a reality, it would break Hinna's heart and would split the entire family. In spite of both sides' refusal to entertain the idea, Youssef told Dalal he was willing to elope with her. She thought about it for a few days but finally told him, as she sobbed into his chest, "I love you, but I just can't cut myself off from my family and my community and live like a pariah."

Although they agreed to remain friends, it didn't work—romantic love doesn't turn into friendship just by virtue of changing a relationship's designation. Soon enough, her father got wind of the fact that they were still seeing each other and he used his connections to distance Youssef from his beloved. Within a couple of months, a ministerial decree was issued transferring Dalal to an entirely different department of the Ministry of Agriculture. They met a few more times but eventually decided to break it off. About a year and a half later, he was so overcome with longing for her that he left work half an hour early and began driving around the area of her new office on the off chance of catching a glimpse of her. His heart missed several beats and felt as if it had landed in his stomach when he caught sight of her standing in front of the building, her belly swollen. A car stopped to pick her up a few moments later and Dalal got in next to a man, probably the person whose baby she was carrying.

Youssef sank into a deep depression. He'd known that she couldn't be his, that they couldn't be together, but the sight of her pregnant brought it home brutally: never again would she be his Dalal. This image of her haunted him for months afterward, but in time memory of her pregnant belly dissipated and was replaced by images of Dalal inhaling the scent of the Arabian jasmine flowers which he used to bring her, or of her smile as she sat beside him in the car with her hair fluttering in the wind echoing the flutter of his heart. He never found out what became of her: he didn't know whether she was still in Iraq or had joined the ranks of the diaspora; he didn't even know if she was still alive.

Living in the Past

1

I decided it was time for my monthly visit with Saadoun. I'd been missing him recently, and he was the last of my friends who was still alive. We'd met at a soccer match decades earlier; it was the 1979 game between al-Zawraa and al-Minaa at al-Shaab stadium. We were seated next to each other in the covered section during the unfortunate match when al-Zawraa's star, Falah Hassan, was injured and broke his leg. In the middle of the second half, Falah was alone in the penalty area when al-Minaa's goalie ran toward him to cut him off. To avoid hitting the goalie's head with his foot, Falah leapt into the air in a half-twist and fell to the ground, immobilized. When Thamir Youssef, his offense teammate, approached and saw his mangled leg, he buried his head in his hands and wept. Players from both teams gathered around the injured star. The entire crowd stood up on the bleachers and a stunned silence descended over the stadium. Many people cried that day, as Falah was a star of international repute and Iraq's most famous player. They laid him on a stretcher, carried him to the ambulance that had driven onto the field from a side entrance, and whisked him away to Medical City Hospital.

Our passion for al-Zawraa and our distress over Abu Taysir, as Falah was known, brought us together, and during our first conversation we commiserated about the fate of his career and the future of the club without his offensive skills.

Even though al-Zawraa ended up winning that match by one goal, Saadoun was somber. Speaking loud enough for all the spectators around to hear, he announced, "This is a complete disaster. Tonight, I'm getting drunk!"

I agreed with him, "It really merits a bender."

At the end of the game, we headed out together, walking alongside the large crowd of spectators spilling out toward Andalus Square as we commiserated. We went into the first bar we found and spent the next three hours there, drinking and talking. We went over every one of Falah's offensive plays and all his best goals; we bemoaned his misfortune and al-Zawraa's bad luck—his injury was obviously serious and we were sure he would never again return to the field even though he was at the height of his form. In spite of it all, I was determined that we should part on an optimistic note.

"To Abu Taysir's health—may he recover and come back stronger!" I exclaimed, raising my glass in one last toast.

Fully agreeing with my sentiment, Saadoun began repeating the words like an incantation to the wine gods. Falah Hassan went to Britain for treatment and *al-Watan* sports magazine ran a photo spread of him exercising with the British physiotherapy team helping with his rehab. He was back six months later, and at the first match he played at al-Shaab stadium he got down on his knees and kissed the ground before the start of play. Saadoun and I went to the game together, having become fast friends in the intervening months. That day, Saadoun teared up as he yelled at the top of his lungs, "I'll lay my life down for that golden orb," referring to Falah's bald head.

In those days, Saadoun was a high school Arabic teacher, and he also ran a small stationery shop in Karrada that he and his brother, Salih, had inherited from their father. He invited me to join the al-Khayyam Society and attend its weekly meetings at the eponymous Khayyam Hotel whose bar he described as "Abu Nuwas Central"—an evening of bacchanalia in the best tradition of Abu Nuwas, the doyen of classical Arabic poetry devoted to hedonism. Ever the master of neologisms and witty sobriquets, Saadoun referred to himself as the group's 'founding leader' both because he was its most ardent supporter and had introduced the merry band of revelers to each other.

The very first time I attended one of these revelries, I understood that the term 'society' was something of an overstatement, reflecting Saadoun's proclivity for exaggeration and verbal prowess. I was the third member of an entire membership of three, the second being Shawqi, Saadoun's colleague who taught biology at the same school. Not much of a drinker or a talker, Shawqi was a portly man who invariably wolfed down the mezze that always came with our drinks. Saadoun teased him about it mercilessly, "Come on, man, demolishing the mezze in one fell swoop! We are going to dinner later, you know."

At first, Saadoun said I couldn't become a full and effective member of the society until I had demonstrated my devotion through regular attendance and confirmed my commitment by drinking the minimum amount of alcohol—three large bottles of beer or their equivalent in araq—over a period of four weeks. Since I was a seasoned drinker, that wasn't too much of a challenge.

The membership might grow to four or even five, on occasion. People came and went as they pleased. For me, it wasn't difficult to be a regular as the hotel was close to the house and I could walk there and back if I had to. Over the years, I became a fixture of the 'society,' along with the other unshakable element, namely Saadoun's irreverent wit—he animated our revelries with his jokes and tales, and his declamations of poetry, especially the wine songs of Abu Nuwas, which he knew by heart and could recite at will. Whenever a waiter passed our table with a tray full of beer bottles, he would declaim a verse or two.

Golden-hued wine, whose abode sorrow never visits,
And whose merest touch gives joy to a rock

or

Ramadan is past and gone,
Bring the cup, O cupbearer,
A lover longing for another.

And when this failed to get the waiter's attention, he would remonstrate loudly,

O cupbearer, to you our complaint is directed
You hear us not, and still we call on you.

Following the so-called Faith Campaign in 1994 when all the bars were shut down, these drinking jags moved into our homes.

"Sons of bitches," Saadoun exclaimed wryly, "taking us back to the days of the underground struggle, making us drink in secret!"

I offered to host and Hinna outdid herself with the mezze she produced for us, especially the boiled beets that I love, and the lablabi of chickpeas swimming in oil and vinegar. Sadly, there were no roasted nut mixes to be had in those days because they had become prohibitively expensive. Our gatherings became more spaced out, and we met once or twice a month sometimes, rather than weekly. In the last years of the Khayyam Society, it was just Saadoun and me. We were no longer a legal assemblage, he liked repeating, because that required a minimum of three people, and then he would segue into the Bard's famous couplet, "Greetings, O carousers, I am intoxicated." His plaintive recitation was neither logical nor rational, I objected, "Can't we have just one carouser? You could just say 'ya nadeemi,' that's all that's needed!"

"Of course not," he answered. "It wouldn't work with one. We must have two. 'Pour me a cup you two. For I miss it like the weaned infant misses suckling nipples.'"

"So why not use 'ya nadeemi' then?"

He would answer me by quoting a segment from the "Long Poem" of al-Jawahiri by the same name. Al-Jawahiri was at the pinnacle of the 'Saadoun encyclopedia' as he liked to refer to his memory while pointing to his head. Al-Jawahiri was his favorite poet of all time. In his estimation, he placed even ahead of al-Mutanabbi, and Saadoun had committed dozens of his poems to memory. "The entire history of Iraq is contained in his diwan," he would tell me.

But decades of drinking took a toll on his health. Medical tests in Baghdad and later in Amman revealed that he had cirrhosis of the liver. To alleviate the severe pain that he likened to being stabbed in the back with knives, he had to give up alcohol, something he initially resisted. He obstinately held to the belief that some trick or stratagem existed which would dispense him from the prohibition. But he eventually came around because he was, "in no hurry to enter hell," as he liked to joke. After that, his drinking was limited to qahwa, the coffee whose increased consumption the doctor encouraged. He comforted himself with the thought that in the qahwa he drank the old meaning of what the Arabs called wine was present.

Two years into the sanctions regime his younger brother, Salih, convinced Saadoun that they should close down the stationery store since they were making nothing but losses. Salih was a smart businessman—he knew how to turn a situation to his advantage and his cleverness paid off handsomely. He wanted to construct a five-story building, with commercial spaces on the ground floor and apartments on the remaining floors, the rent from which would provide a stable income. Saadoun left Salih to do whatever he pleased because, although Saadoun had absolutely no business savvy, he understood all too well that the project would guarantee more security than his schoolteacher's pension, which was a joke. The project would be an asset for him and his children who were all that he had left since his wife had been claimed by cancer two years after the 1991 Gulf War.

I had called Saadoun half an hour earlier but he rarely ever answered his cell phone. I dialed his landline and when his youngest daughter, Sundus, picked up and told me her father was bathing, I asked her to let him know that his nadeem was on his way. After her two brothers and their families had left the country a few years earlier, Sundus, her husband, and their three children had moved into the old family house so that she could take care of her father. The boys had tried to convince Saadoun to come along but he, like me, wouldn't hear of leaving Iraq, and Sundus was determined to remain by his side.

As I approached the front gate, I heard the thrumming of the electric generator from the garden. I rang the bell with my thumb. I looked up at the tall mulberry tree in the garden, which had stood to the right of the gate for decades. It had lost all its leaves and was completely bare. I wondered if the tree could feel the cold that I was beginning to feel. I remembered the palm sapling that I had given Saadoun about two years into our friendship after chiding him about not having any date palms in his garden, and how it had died during a particularly cold winter even though he had wrapped it with coarsely woven burlap rice bags as well as sheets of plastic. The sapling that he got the following year had survived, and it towered magnificently above the far side of the garden. I wondered if the date palm ever addressed the mulberry tree, or whether it was too proud for that? My daydreaming was interrupted by the sound of the door opening. Nine-year-old Aws, Saadoun's youngest grandchild, stepped out and came toward the gate exclaiming, "Welcome, Uncle, welcome!"

"Hey Aws, how are you doing, son? No school today?" I asked.

"No, Uncle, there is school, but I'm not feeling well."

"Salamtak. What's wrong?"

"Nothing serious. I woke up feeling sick this morning, but I'm fine now."

Aws drew back the metal bolt and opened the gate. I kissed him, tousled his black hair, and after he had closed the gate behind me and we were walking toward the house, I asked, "You were sick for real, or just faking it?"

His grandfather, who was standing at the front door, answered on his behalf.

"He's nothing but a trickster and a rascal. He just wanted to stay home with his grandpa. So good to see you, ya nadeemi!"

Even though it had been years since we'd had a drink, Saadoun still called me his drinking companion.

In his right hand was the small comb with which he always and ever-so-carefully combed his remaining white hair and thick moustache. He slipped the comb into his trouser pocket and opened his arms wide to embrace me. He was wearing an open-necked gray sweater over a black shirt, with matching trousers and socks that were visible from the tip of his slippers.

"Hey, what's with being dressed to the nines?" I teased.

"In your honor, of course!"

We hugged and kissed on both cheeks.

"Aws, go tell your mom to make us some coffee," he told his grandson as he showed me into the living room.

Over coffee, which Sundus brought in a quarter of an hour later, he sensed that there was something lurking behind the smiles and the short answers that I was giving him, and he looked quizzical. I was contemplating the delicate design on the white coffee cup in silence when he asked me, "What's up with you today? You're not yourself . . . what's wrong?"

"Nothing's wrong."

"No, something *is* wrong."

"Nothing, really," I went on after a pause. "I just can't get Hinna out of my mind. Today is the anniversary of her death."

His hazel eyes glimmered with sadness, and he shook his head slowly, back and forth, the way he did whenever he was moved by the pleasures of the world or wrenched by its sorrows.

"That's right. . . . May her pure spirit have found everlasting peace," he said.

"Likewise, for your dear departed, Saadoun. And may God bless and protect that little boy."

"How many years is it now? Six, isn't it?"

"Seven."

"Seven years already? It feels like yesterday!"

Silence descended on the room, broken only by the whine of the generator and the sound of Aws arguing with his mother in the other room. "Why, mama, tell me why," he kept repeating loudly.

"You going to church today?" Saadoun asked.

"Yes, of course."

"You know that if it weren't for the fact that I have a doctor's appointment, I would go with you. But it's my regular checkup, and I can't postpone it."

He had attended Hinna's memorial service and the funeral, and had walked by my side as a pallbearer and helped me lower her coffin into the earth. At the service, he'd sat in the front pew and read the opening verse of the Quran, the Fatiha, twice, as some of the attendance looked on puzzled. It wasn't the first time he'd entered a church, he'd also been there when Mikhail and Habiba had died.

"Thank you, my friend. I will light a candle on your behalf," I said, tremulously.

"Yes, please do. She was like a sister to me. May the Lord's mercy be hers."

Another silence followed.

"Tell me, something. Do you think I'm living in the past?" I asked him.

"Who ever said such a thing?"

"Maha, my relative. The one who lives upstairs with her husband."

"Well, of course, there's a grain of truth in it. We're antiquated old things. Like that little rascal Aws said the other day, 'Grandpa, you're so ancient!'"

I laughed and told him about my dream. "I dreamed that the house had become a museum, and that I worked there as a docent, taking people on tours of the rooms."

He chuckled heartily. "Oh, that's a good one," he said. "In that case, I'm going to be coming over to punch visitors' tickets at the door! Tell me, what was the occasion for her saying that?"

"We'd been discussing sectarianism and our status as Christians, and before I knew it, we were arguing and the argument became very heated."

"So what? A disagreement should never come between friends."

"I know, but the disagreement was profound. She's very pessimistic . . . she thinks there's no hope left for us in this country. She just wants to get her degree and leave with her husband."

"She's right. How can you blame her? She's in the same boat as hundreds of thousands of people who've left. Let them go and try somewhere else. They have the grit necessary and their lives are in front of them. Isn't she the one who miscarried?"

"Yes, that's right."

"Poor thing—she's heartsick. She's a thakla, a bereaved mother."

Exaggerating his enunciation, Saadoun went on, "Thakla, thakla, my drinking companion. Haven't you heard what the thakla says to her son?" He spread his right hand wide open and covered his eyes with his palm. This was a signal that poetry was on his lips. His voice was sonorous as he intoned:

O wound in my heart, entrails, and liver
Would that your mother had never conceived or given birth
When I saw you enshrouded
Embalmed for rest until eternity's end. . . .

He faltered at the next verse.

"And then what? . . . Hmmm . . . then . . . ?" he asked, speaking to himself. He was quiet for a moment and then repeated the second verse to jog his memory. He tapped his forehead a few times, and when he recovered what he'd been searching for, he lowered his hand. "That's it, yes, I've got it. . . . 'I knew that after you, life would not go on, / For how shall the forearm live stripped of its upper portion?'"

On hearing beautiful poetry, I exhaled a deep sigh of satisfaction. This was always a spontaneous reaction, but sometimes I'd add a word or phrase of appreciation. I loved the gems that Saadoun regaled me with and I was astounded by his memory, which had hardly rusted after all these years. As I often did, I asked who the poet was.

"Unknown," he replied. "A mother whose heart was seared in pre-Islamic times."

"But that was about a son that had been born and had grown before her eyes, when she lost him."

"Yes, it was. But still, my friend, it's not easy. He was her flesh and blood! And one more thing, not everyone is an optimist like you. Tell me, where do you get all your optimism? Who's going to save us from that band of thugs, crooks, and turban heads? It's been almost a year, and they still haven't formed a government—a *year*!"

"The turbans will unravel, in due course. But that girl, Maha . . . she doesn't believe there was a time when sectarianism didn't exist."

Saadoun sighed and said, "By the time the turbans unravel, we will be dead and buried. That is, if they do. Between Iranians, Arabs, and Americans, our country has been decimated. Honestly, it's still a mystery to me. Has there been sectarianism all along and we simply weren't aware of it? Is that even possible? Where was it lurking all that time? Or is it all a result of foreign interference and this hatred for us, and all those people returning from abroad who brought all their filth with them? Take Sundus, for example, isn't she married to a Shiite? Was that a problem fifteen years ago?"

I remembered a sectarian joke that Luay had told me a week earlier.

"Listen, you're going to like this one," I said. "Three Iraqis, one Sunni, one Shiite, and one Christian, get hold of a magic lamp. The genie pops out and asks the Shiite guy, 'What is your wish? Ask and it shall be done.' 'Get rid of all the Sunnis,' the man answers. 'Every last one of them!' 'It shall be so,' the genie replies. Then he turns to the Sunni and asks him for his wish. The man says, 'Kill all the Shiites so that not one of them remains alive.' And the genie again answers, 'It shall be so.' When he turns to the third man and asks him the same question, the Christian says, 'Take care of those guys' wishes first and then come back to me.'"

We laughed until tears streamed down our face.

"What a rascal," Saadoun said. "That was a good one!"

I changed the subject and we got to talking about Falah Hassan, our favorite player, who had just returned to Iraq to head the al-Zawraa Club and help it rebuild after years of hardship. I asked Saadoun if he had heard the news that Falah intended to run for the presidency of the Iraqi soccer federation.

"For real?" he said.

"Yeah, I saw it in the paper a couple of days ago."

"Well, there's no one more qualified. Let's hope it's true. But tell me what's Abu Taysir got to do with sectarianism and your relative?"

"Nothing. There's nothing more to say. Case closed. I'm sure she'll apologize—it only happened last night."

"Hope springs eternal."

Saadoun dropped the subject and we talked for another hour or so. But then he brought it up again in a backhanded sort of way when we were having lunch—delicious rice and okra stew studded with fat garlic cloves just the way I like it, along with a salad, all made by his daughter, and fresh tannour bread from the bakery nearby. We got around to discussing the government crisis and the rise of sectarian tension in the country.

"Do you know what al-Jawahiri said on the subject of sectarianism?" he asked, pouring me some water.

"No. What'd he say?"

"Ay TarTara taTarTari, Brag and boast, Go forward, go backwards, / Be Shiite, be Sunni, be Jewish or Christian, Kurdish or Arab."

"Yeah, he said that a long time ago, didn't he? Does that mean that this whole time there's been sectarianism?"

"Of course, man, we've always had Sunnis and Shiites, Christians and Muslims, but not massacres and extermination, militias, and car bombs."

"Heaven help us."

The ditty kept drumming through my head as I walked home after I left him. "Ay TarTara taTarTari . . . ."

2

On my way back, I passed by a house whose owners were obviously neglecting the date palm in their courtyard, neither pollinating nor pruning it. I was reminded of Brisam, the date palm climber, or saaud, who'd pruned and pollinated our trees for more than thirty years. He would have been hopping mad at the sight. Brisam would wander along the streets of residential neighborhoods and ring on doorbells whenever he saw a date palm that looked neglected. He'd ring until someone answered the door and would then give them a piece of his mind, berating them for being heartless and mean. In his last years, when he was almost deaf, he went around declaiming at the top of his lungs: "All I have are God and the date palms . . . only God and the date palms!"

Sometimes, you'd hear him shouting, "This one is a Barhi!"

God loved him for sure: he took Brisam to his eternal rest one day around noon after the saaud had shimmied up a tree to pollinate it. Brisam's arms were wrapped around the tree trunk and his body was held aloft in a brace when his heart simply came to a stop.

He died caring for a tree to which he spoke as if it were a human being. According to Jasim, who looked after our two trees after Brisam died, he had become a legend among the date palm climbers. Jasim wasn't much of a talker. Whenever I asked how the trees were doing, he gave me a reply that was both vague and terse, "Thanks be to God, sir! Everything is going as it should."

The only time he ever let loose was three years ago when he rang the bell and told me that he'd decided not to work as a saaud that season because he was going back to his village. I asked him why.

"I'm going back home," he said. "These days, when I knock, people I've never seen before in my life come to the door. Some of them say they're relatives of the owners, that they're looking out for the house, but that's baloney. When I ask them where the owners have gone, they don't have an answer. Anyhow, it's none of my business. Did you know that twelve of us have been killed? Better for me to go home and work in the orchards down south. It's safer over there."

People had stopped giving him keys to let himself into their courtyards and tend to the trees while they slept, or when no one was home. Now, when the women and girls of the household were there alone, they wouldn't allow him in and would tell him to come back when one of the men was home.

"Honestly, I was better off before the Americans came . . . I could go and come as I pleased. I could sleep under a tree or in a corner anywhere and no one bothered me. Now I have to get a room in a hostel or else get killed. And the massive concrete blast walls are suffocating us. I swear to God, even the date palms are Sunni and Shiite now. I have to leave my bicycle at the checkpoint, I can't take it in with me—that was before it got stolen, of course. The dates are wilted and dying of thirst. Do you know how many trees have been cut and burned so that the Americans can see the snipers and the snipers can see them? That is what it has come to. Ya haram, it's such a shame."

I was pained by his words, but not surprised—I'd always maintained that the date palm was the weathervane for human affairs. The fortunes of the two were inextricably linked. What befell humans was a reflection of the tree's condition, and war didn't differentiate between the heads of men and the crowns of the tree: it decapitated them both.

In that they are created male and female, humans resemble palm trees. Only after it is pollinated by her male counterpart does the female tree become fertile and hang heavy with fruit that is clustered in large and heavy bunches. Like an infant, a palm sapling must be protected from the cold and the rain in order for it to grow strong.

I wondered if the owners of the house I had just passed had fled. Or perhaps the current occupants were just indifferent to the trees. Was there such a thing as an Iraqi who didn't love the date palm? I was certain that those who had no love for the date palm had no love for life or their fellow human beings.

From a distance, the fronds of the two date palms towering above our garden seemed to me to be protecting the house—and I, too, was guarding it along with all the memories it contained. The house was more than a mere shelter, it was like a palm tree, which isn't a mere tree but a living being unto itself, joined with the earth beneath it, the sky above it, and the air around it which it breathed. So, too, the house, which wasn't merely a combination of bricks, mortar, and paint, but the assemblage of an entire lifetime.

"It would be best to sell the house and leave," Amal had said through her tears, when she called after Hinna died. "Things are going to go from bad to worse. Why stay there on your own? You can come here or go and live with Salima in Sweden. Please Youssef, I beg you to leave."

I responded the way I always had.

"I'm not leaving," I told her. "I'm not going anywhere at my age—I'm too old for such humiliation."

Many a real estate broker had been knocking on my door lately, to ask if I was thinking of selling. And my answer was always no. Our neighborhood was considered one of the safer and calmer areas in the city and prices were going up. A few upscale restaurants had opened and the nouveaux riches had begun buying up old houses that they then tore down and replaced with ostentatious mansions.

One evening, as we were watching television, Luay asked me if I'd ever considered leaving.

"At my age? Better suffer here than experience the humiliations of being a refugee. If I were young, I would consider it. It's different for you and Maha—your lives are ahead of you, you can go and start over in a new place. I'm not going anywhere. I built this house, and I've lived in it for more than half a century. How could I leave it?"

"Have you ever had the opportunity?"

"I did once or twice. I got an offer from Abu Dhabi in the late seventies, and another one from Dubai in 1989. I turned them both down."

"Do you ever regret it?"

"No. D'you know what al-Gubbanchi says?"

"What?"

"'Do not think that in leaving there is comfort
I see nothing in it but grief and weariness,
All sleep was robbed from my eyes.
I never thought and no one knew
That it would be like this.'"

3

After translating the book, which the agency then published, I got a promotion and received a hefty raise. I dedicated myself completely to work and within three years, I had saved enough money to buy a good piece of land near Karrada where I wanted to build a new home for the family. Habiba had returned from Sulaymaniya to work in Baghdad and was betrothed to her first cousin on our mother's side. She moved in with him at his parents' house in al-Sinak, and then they got a place of their own. She offered to contribute to the costs of building the new house as a gift to our father—she wanted him to be comfortable in his old age and to be surrounded by his sons and daughters, and any grandchildren that were on the way. Although we both agreed that his name should be on the deed, he objected vehemently, and so we registered the house in Hinna's name.

Just as I recall the day I planted the palm saplings at opposite ends of the backyard, I also remember when there was nothing but the foundations back in 1955. I would come by every week to check on the progress of the work and Khalaf, the foreman in charge, would brief me. On one of my visits some months into the work, I was surprised to see that they had used palm fronds to build the arch that the architect had designed for the reception room. When Khalaf assured me that it was an old and time-tested technique, I remembered seeing pictures in the book about date palms and the way the inhabitants of the marshes built similar structures in their guest quarters and their houses.

The house was on a lovely quiet street near the Opera Gardens that was later named after Jaafar Ali al-Tayyar, a prominent man who lived in the first house ever to be built on the street. The main thoroughfare it branched onto became known as Street 42. This was because people called the next street over from the main thoroughfare Street 52, after the bus that plied that route, and that was the roundabout way in which the streets in the vicinity were numbered.

I entrusted the design of the house to a friend from Baghdad College who'd gone abroad to study architecture and had come back and started his own firm. My main instruction was that the house had to be spacious enough to accommodate the entire family. Thus, we had six bedrooms, three on each of the two floors, a large reception lounge for entertaining guests, and an everyday living room. The architect suggested having a fireplace in the reception room and I agreed enthusiastically. There was a small yard at the front of the house, and a very large one at the back.

The blooms on the bougainvillea whose branches scaled the façade of the house came into view. In addition to its heat hardiness and its ability to bloom year-round, I had chosen it for the beauty of its flowers, which looked like so many vermilion tongues licking at a fire. From the distance, I could also see the crowns of the three Seville orange trees that I had planted in the garden at the front. How I love the smell of those oranges! There's really nothing like it. Whenever the harvest season came around, I'd pick and juice the oranges in the kitchen, and Hinna would freeze the juice to use in her cooking. I did this every year, even after she was gone. I would offer a container of frozen bitter orange juice to any visitors that dropped by. Nothing else flavors food like the juice of bitter oranges, I'd tell them, and I had no use for it.

I looked up toward the upstairs bedroom windows. The curtains were drawn which meant Maha wasn't home. I noticed that the metal plaque hanging on the pillar to the right of the gate that had my name on it was so dusty that the Y was hardly visible. I wiped my finger across the plaque—it really needed polishing. I opened the gate and bent down to turn on the water spigot close by. I took out a pack of tissues from my pocket, pulled three out, wetted them with a few drops of water and stepped back out to clean the plaque. Although my lower back hurt, I was pleased that I had cleaned my name, and I cursed at the proliferation of dust and soot in recent years. I remembered that the myrtle tree between the garage and the garden needed pruning. I would ask Luay to do it when he could.

Once inside the house, I realized how tired I felt and that I needed to make up for the previous night's broken sleep. I got undressed and went to bed.

4

Even though I was alone in the house, I could hear water running as if someone were bathing. Going toward the bathroom, I heard the sound of a woman singing an unfamiliar pop song. Outside the door, which had been left ajar, I recognized it was Maha singing. I wondered why she had come down here instead of using the upstairs bathroom. From where I stood, all I could see was the very wet floor. She stopped singing, and called out my name.

"Youssef, come in. Open the door. Don't be shy, come on in."

How did she know I was standing outside the door? Had she heard my footsteps? This was the first time she hadn't called me 'Uncle.' . . . I pushed the door open and saw her standing naked under the shower rocking a baby in her arms. The shower curtain had disappeared and water was streaming down her hair and shoulders onto the floor. She was trying to get the infant to latch onto the raised nipple of one of her breasts, which were round and rosy as pomegranates. The infant didn't stir, he seemed fast asleep. I wondered how he could sleep with all the water and the noise around him. Maha looked at me and smiled; she showed no sign of embarrassment and didn't try to cover up her nakedness.

"Come in Youssef," she repeated. "Come close and look at how beautiful my baby is. I'm going to baptize him."

Had she lost her mind? She was going to baptize this strange child in this bathroom? Where had she found him? Would she get angry if I told her he wasn't her son? I looked for a towel with which to cover her, but as soon as I stepped into the bathroom, I slipped on the wet floor and fell.

I wiped the sweat from my forehead as I was startled awake, feeling guilty about the visions in my dream. For me, Maha was like a daughter and I certainly didn't want to think of her in that way. That kind of thing wasn't much on my mind anymore—after being loud and insistent, my sexual urges had abated and no longer rattled my bones on a daily basis, the way they used to. But I have to admit that the feelings of the man had superseded those of the father on two or three occasions already. . . . Once, when her nipples stood up under a see-through top she wore on a very hot day . . . and another time, when I looked out of the window and saw her sitting on the patio swing in the backyard, with her legs crossed and her thighs showing. My paternal feelings truly vanished the time I came across her waxing her legs. I was on my way to the roof that day because I had noticed that every time I turned on the water, it smelled putrid, and I thought there might be a dead pigeon in the rooftop tank, as sometimes happened. To get up there, I had to go through their apartment on the top floor. I hadn't realized that Maha had come home early from university. I opened the door to the apartment and there she was sitting on the ground, her legs splayed wide open, dressed in skimpy white shorts and a tank top without a bra underneath. She was holding a small square of fabric and a jar of wax was on the floor with more fabric squares stacked beside it. She snapped her legs shut and scrambled to her feet, visibly shaken. I shut the door quickly and apologized. "I'm sorry, I didn't know anyone was home," I called out. "I was going up to the roof. I'll come back later."

I got out of bed, slipped something onto my feet, and went to the kitchen for a drink of water. Maha wasn't in the bathroom when I went to wash my face, as she had been in the dream. Dabbing my face dry, I thought about the fact that she and her husband would be leaving in a few months, and how I would remain alone after they were gone. I went back to the kitchen to put the kettle on, I really needed some tea. I would certainly be able to find someone to whom I could rent the upper floor but I would miss them. Especially Maha. Her husband was nice, he was a polite and helpful young man, but he was at work most of the time. It was with her that I interacted the most and she was clearly interested in getting to know me better. It didn't feel as if her interest was just a matter of being polite and repaying my hospitality—it resulted from a true closeness that had grown between us in spite of our disagreements. She had suggested I set up an email account and had helped me to do it. At first, I'd said no, I didn't have a computer and wasn't going to buy one, but she offered to let me use her laptop. She taught me how to get into my account and send messages to my sisters. She wrote down the instructions for me on a piece of paper, including the username and password, *yusif1933* and *zahdi*. She laughed when I told her what I wanted the password to be.

"It's always dates and palm trees with you!" she exclaimed.

I was so thrilled by the new discovery that I immediately sent my sister two messages. But it wasn't long before I decided it was better to talk on the phone after all—I couldn't keep track of the various steps and found it all slow going.

Maha was also the one who showed me new pictures of relatives on Facebook. And she's the one who introduced me to a YouTube page that features recordings of traditional Iraqi maqam music, including rare ones. We'd been talking about classical music and I had told her about my passion for the maqam and the extensive cassette collection of which I was so proud. I didn't know anything about YouTube but she brought the laptop downstairs to show me. Together, we listened to the latest song that had been uploaded to the anthology, inter-preted by Filfil Gurji, and I was astounded.

Maha helped me to get on Skype to talk to my sisters, Amal and Salima, too. The whole thing reminded me of sci-fi films and Star Trek, which used to run on Saturday nights decades ago. I never would have dreamed that one day I'd be able to see a person on a screen as I talked to them on a computer.

On a call to Canada a week ago, my younger sister, Amal, asked me whether I'd arranged a special service in Hinna's memory. I said I had, and that I planned to go to the cemetery the week after the service to place a wreath and pray by her graveside. She asked who would be there.

"Who else besides me, Maha, and her husband?" I replied. She said nothing and then burst into tears. She begged me to sell the house and leave the country, just as she always did whenever we spoke on the phone.

"Why stay in the big house all alone? And who's going to look after you once Maha's gone?"

"Well, didn't I live alone before Maha came here? Don't worry about me, nothing will happen."

"What are you talking about, Youssef? Don't you see how they're killing priests and attacking churches?"

"Who told you I'd become a priest?"

Humor was my sharpest weapon in such conversations, but Amal wasn't amused.

"Right now, everything's fine," I went on. "There've been a few bomb attacks here and there, but they've stopped. Where we are, things are quiet."

The lyrics of a song I hadn't heard in a long time came back to me as I sipped on my tea. It had been ages since I had intoned those words! I picked up the istikan and went to my room to find the recording. I put the tea glass down on the small coffee table and stood in front of the neatly ordered tape collection on the shelf. I glanced over toward the Youssef Omar section, and my eyes fell on the spine of the cover with the words, *Youssef Omar: Maqamat*. Exactly what I'd been looking for! I pulled out the tape and slipped it into the cassette recorder. I must have stopped at the end of the zuhayri last time I listened to it because Omar was singing,

What have I done for you to hurt me so?
Precious as my eyes

73

My heart's desire
Why hurt me so?
Have I wronged you?
Are you weary of me?
Of vexation, enough
Be kind, I beseech you
Relinquish your displeasure.

In the intervals between verses, a collective moan of pleasure swelled up from the audience. The musician's fingers plucked the santour as if enumerating all the sorrows the lyrics and melody invoked before handing over to the singer once again.

O my heart, dissolve and melt, wail and break into pieces
O my eyes, let the tears fall from your reddened eyelids
Weep, my soul, and weep again
Weep for those who left you
You who left so distressed
Tell me, what is your wish?
Whatever it is, I will do as you wish
Your love rules
It is him my heart loves
What is it to others? Each to his own
My love left me and went away
Who will bring him back?
I will never implore him or his beloved
Weep, my soul, and weep again
Weep for those who left you
The key to the heart
Is gone and lost at sea
Not even Job was as patient
As I was with you.

I was close to tears, but pulled myself together. Why was I choking up? Because I felt sad about Hinna, because I was upset with Maha, or maybe both? Perhaps it was just life itself: the things that had been done as well as those that were left undone. These songs, and the maqams in particular, were like secret passageways to the soul and I meandered through them alone, between wondrous walls held together by an invisible mortar that was a mix of sadness and longing, and I peered through their windows listening for another song or for the sound of silence. I spent a couple of hours searching through my cassette library, listening to songs that I loved and hadn't heard in a long time.

After that, I went back to bed because I still felt tired and sleepy. Rather than bemoan the days of my youth, I gave thanks for old age. It gave me permission to be lazy and indolent. Old age gave its subject the liberty of taking more than one nap for no good reason. I had worked hard all my life and now I had a right to be lazy.

5

From my bedroom window, the courtyard looked forlorn. I had picked the last jasmine flower three weeks earlier. It was fall, and everything was in mourning. It would all be reborn in spring, I told myself as I dressed to go to church, because everything is born again. The carnations, the climbing roses, and the snapdragons would fill the garden with color again. In the warmth of the spring sun I would again sit on the patio swing and drink tea, close my eyes and smell the flowers. Everything would bloom again, that is, everything except for Hinna. Her grave wouldn't bloom again because autumn is the only season that the dead know. Nothing but autumn, until the Resurrection. . . . How long until I took my place next to Hinna and the others, I wondered? To secure my spot on this last journey and to spare others the burden, I'd already paid the Rahma Association for all the expenses related to my passing—the coffin, the burial, as well as the church service.

I was by no means convinced about the resurrection of the body. I just didn't see how a collection of bones can rise up and reclaim the flesh and skin that covered them. If that were true, the world would turn into a zombie movie. But a person's spirit is another matter and I did believe it doesn't die. Where it goes, I wasn't sure. Who knows, I might end up being a bird flitting from courtyard to courtyard—and still get to eat dates. I might even end up coming back to this house and living right beside my beloved palm trees. The idea that death offered the body eternal rest and the spirit a new birth was very appealing and it soothed my heart. Hinna's spirit would be either in Jerusalem or in Rome. And who knows, she might even come back to her room or step into the dome of the church when she heard her name being spoken and the angels told her that her renegade brother was praying for her eternal rest.

6

I dressed in a light blue shirt and black trousers and put on my walking shoes and the jacket I had worn in the morning to go and see Saadoun. I heard the sound of movement upstairs. Was Maha back? Perhaps she'd come down and apologize? If not, I would see her in the courtyard of the church after the service. I decided to walk there, it was only twenty or twenty-five minutes away, and taking the car was a nuisance because of all the checkpoints in the area around the church. Besides, driving made my back hurt. Today was a day for walking, I decided, and I could always come back with Maha and her husband.

Reaching the end of the street, I passed the building where Artine's used to be—I bought my coffee there for over twenty years but then he too closed up shop and left the country. It became a chicken rotisserie place and even though I loved chicken, I missed the smell of roasting beans laced with crushed cardamom. I turned right onto the main thoroughfare and the National Theater building loomed into view on the left. When I bought the plot of land on which I built the house, it was rumored that an opera venue was being planned for the site, but the project never saw the light of day. Beautiful gardens had been created where people still strolled in the evenings, but instead of an opera house, the National Theater was built. In long-gone days, I occasionally went and saw a play there or attended a classical music concert.

I passed by what used to be known as the Opera Gardens across from the air force command. Four more streets and I would turn left and then go straight all the way to the church. Another fifteen minutes, and the high arch bearing the distinctive cross inside a circle loomed into view. Walking toward the church building, I noticed that the palm tree in the courtyard had grown taller, its upper fronds practically embracing the cross. I was early and there weren't many people making their way to church yet. A guard stopped me at the entrance but he didn't search me and was satisfied when I said I was a Christian coming to attend a service.

"Please come in," he said respectfully.

I walked toward the little stone grotto enclosing a statue of the Virgin Mary in the courtyard behind the church. Two women stood reverentially to one side. I took out a few bills from my wallet and placed them inside a wooden money box on which were painted in white the words *Association of Our Lady of Deliverance for the Aid of the Poor*. I lit a taper from the pile stacked next to the box, and anchored it on the tray next to six others that were already burning. Then I lit one more on behalf of Saadoun, as I had promised, and looked toward the statue. A sudden gust of wind ruffled the flames and I had to relight a candle that had gone out.

I heard the rustling of the palm fronds above my head and felt happy that a palm tree was in the courtyard to protect Mary inside her grotto. Hinna and I had had an argument on the very subject some twenty years earlier. We'd been sitting having our tea in front of the television one evening when

Abdel-Basit began chanting Surat Maryam, a splendid calligraphy of which was displayed on the screen.

And the pangs of childbirth drove her unto the trunk of the palm-tree. She said: Oh, would that I had died ere this and had become a thing of naught, forgotten!
Then (one) cried unto her from below her, saying: Grieve not! Thy Lord hath placed a rivulet beneath thee,
And shake the trunk of the palm-tree toward thee, thou wilt cause ripe dates to fall upon thee.
So eat and drink and be consoled.

Hinna began muttering the way she did when she was irked.

"What I'd like to know is where Muhammad got this palm tree story from? There's nothing of the sort in the Gospels."

"There is actually . . . but not in the version you read."

I had recently read about the Gnostic Gospels and the historical details had impressed me.

"And what gospel would that be?" she asked, puzzled.

"The story of the palm tree and Jesus speaking from his cradle occurs in two gospels the church rejects."

"So why haven't I heard of it?"

"How could you? The church isn't going to tell you about gospels it won't recognize."

"If they were authentic, we would've heard about them long ago."

"What do you mean authentic? They recount stories from the life of Jesus just like the other gospels do. There's a gospel written by Judas and one by Mary Magdalene."

"A gospel written by Judas? Don't be ridiculous."

"It's a historical fact, but the church doesn't want it to be known."

"And what I'd like to know is what business you have with the church? You never set foot there and won't have anything to do with it!"

"Alright, alright, don't get upset. But honestly, why won't you let the Virgin Mary have a few dates?"

Now she was really angry—to her such words were tantamount to blasphemy.

"Honestly, I tell you, Youssef, sometimes you just go too far," she said, getting up and leaving the room.

I felt remorseful because I liked needling her for no reason. I wasn't pious or devout the way she was, but I had faith in my own way. I just didn't put much store by obligations and teachings. I considered them signposts on the path to God for those who needed them—a code of conduct that they felt was necessary, but I felt no such need. I knew that God existed, that the universe and all it encompassed weren't just random occurrences that had no rhyme or reason—even though I still had many questions to which I hadn't found any clear answers. Questions about the universe, about mankind and nature. The question that bothered me in particular was how God could allow all the evil there was without punishing its perpetrators, despite being omnipresent—not just in holy books, prayers, and houses of worship, but in nature, in beauty. It didn't matter to me which of the many paths to God people followed. The path itself was no guarantee of the seeker's purity, in any case. People, both good and bad, trod the path to God, and some thought theirs was the only true way.

I made the sign of the cross and turned around. A young woman in her twenties, with deep black eyes and a gorgeous face, wearing a blue dress and carrying a black purse to match her shoes, was leaning against the trunk of one of the tall palm trees. She had slipped off one of her shoes apparently to relieve a painful foot. She looked down at her reddened heel and then said to an older woman who could've been her mother but who wasn't as nicely dressed, "Go on in ahead of me . . . I'll be there in a minute." The older woman headed toward the church entrance, and I followed suit.

I went up the three wide steps and entered. I dipped my index finger in the glass of holy water and made the sign of the cross on my face. I walked down the aisle between the wooden pews toward the altar. The chandeliers hanging from the ceiling hadn't been turned on yet, there was enough light coming in through the large windows high up on the walls. Engraved in gold Kufic script, the words of the Credo glowed on the wooden molding that framed the arcade of columns running the entire length of the nave. I had learned the words by heart when I was a child, repeating them and hearing them repeated at every church service.

> *I believe in one God,*
> *the Father Almighty,*
> *maker of heaven and earth,*
> *and of all things visible and invisible;*
> *And in one Lord Jesus Christ,*
> *the only begotten Son of God,*
> *begotten of his Father before all worlds,*
> *God of God, Light of Light,*
> *very God of very God,*
> *begotten, not made,*
> *being of one substance with the Father;*
> *by whom all things were made;*
> *who for us and for our salvation came down from heaven,*
> *and was incarnate by the Holy Ghost of the Virgin Mary,*
> *and was made man;*
> *and was crucified also for us*
> *under Pontius Pilate;*
> *he suffered and was buried;*
> *and the third day he rose again*
> *according to the Scriptures,*
> *and ascended into heaven,*
> *and sitteth on the right hand of the Father;*
> *and he shall come again, with glory,*

to judge both the quick and the dead;
whose kingdom shall have no end.

The columns seemed to be carrying a heavy burden. In addition to the Credo, each pillar bore the weight of the bricks, cement, plaster, and ceiling on top of it, as well as a scene from the Stations of the Cross reproducing the various stages of the Passion, when Christ carried the cross to Golgotha and thence to his fateful destination.

Some twenty people who'd arrived before me were already seated in various places. About six rows from the front, I slipped into a pew on my right, claiming the space nearest the aisle. I made the sign of the cross one more time, and sat down in contemplation. The hushed silence inside the church was broken only by the young man testing the microphones that had been set up for the choir, and by the sound of occasional footfalls, throat clearing, or benches creaking as someone sat down. I took out my phone and saw there were no messages. I had been expecting Maha to call or text me. I turned off the phone—it really bothered me when cell phones rang in inappropriate places and times—and put it back in my pocket.

I looked up at the large paintings hanging on the wall in front of me, right above the altar and directly under the dome. In the center painting, the Blessed Mother, donning a golden crown, extended her hand to all those looking toward her. From a halo of light on her bosom, the child Jesus looked out innocently, clutching his own glowing heart in the left hand while his right hand lay open, palm facing up. To the right of that painting was another in which Mary, dressed in her blue robe and with a white veil on her head, knelt in prayer as a flight of angels circled above her in the sky. To her left knelt an angel larger than the rest that didn't look like an angel at all but more like a man in a white robe with two wings. My gaze moved to the third painting in which the figure of Jesus stood in the center of the heavens in a white tunic and blue robe.

Rays of light radiated from his face and dozens of angels hovered nearby. The vaulted ceiling and sides of the dome were covered in frescoes of celestial spume mingling with ocean waves. Two cherubs holding a crown hovered above the head of the Virgin Mary who was seated inside the sun's orb. She seemed unaware that she was being crowned, her attention directed at the swaddled Jesus lying in her lap.

Even though my attendance was lackadaisical, I appreciated the aesthetics of the church and was moved by its liturgies and rites, especially when the deacon or priest had a melodious voice. The chants, the incense, the bells, the lavishly embroidered vestments, and the prayers all moved my spirit, quite possibly for other reasons than those of most worshippers. For me, the chants in Aramaic and Syriac that the priest intoned issued from the dawn of time, from unknown beginnings. I considered mass a celebration of life, of birth, of death, and of resurrection, not only Christ's, but all of humanity. To me, Christ was an immortal sacred tree that withstood storms and floods and came back to life every spring. I stopped myself because these were the very things that provoked Hinna's fury—such views were anathema, in her opinion, the worst sort of absurdist philosophy, and here I was bringing them to mind at this service in her memory. I remembered how furious she'd been when I once voiced the opinion that Mary's suffering had been greater than Christ's, because she saw her own son being crucified and there was no greater grief than a mother's. Then I started thinking about Maha and her sorrow. I wondered whether my words, and my 'objectivity,' had been too harsh. I needed to avoid such arguments with her in the few remaining months before her departure. The church was getting full and I turned around several times to look for her and Luay but didn't see them anywhere.

Mater Dolorosa

Shake the trunk of this moment
And it will provide death in abundance

—An Iraqi Mary

1

I entered the darkened bedroom, kicked off my house shoes, flung myself on the bed, and buried my face in the cold pillow. It wasn't really *our* bedroom at all but more of a way station. Just like the rest of the house, and our entire life by that point. My grief quickly rose to the surface and spilled out as it had for the whole of the past year, at first a soft keening, and then the tears came in heaving, rhythmic, sobs. I'd forgotten to close the door behind me and they were sure to hear me!

Soon enough, I heard the sound of footsteps coming up the stairs. They got closer, the light was switched on, and Luay's voice repeated my name gently.

"Hey, what's wrong?" he asked.

"Please, please, turn it off!" I cried. The light's harshness felt unbearable. "Please, I'm begging you, turn the light off." I repeated through my tears as I clung to the pillow and covered my eyes to block out the glare.

"As you wish, my love." He switched the light off and closed the door.

He came over to sit on the edge of the bed and I felt his hand on my right shoulder. I didn't move. I was curled up in a

83

fetal position, with my back turned to him. He reached over to wipe the tears from my face, but I just wound myself in more tightly. Even though I felt bad doing it, I couldn't help myself. I couldn't bear being touched. He withdrew his hand and I felt him lie down against my back. He put his arm around me diffidently, without saying anything. As I wept, I wondered whether he was getting fed up with me. He didn't say much anymore, and never uttered a word when I'd get upset or fly into a rage. He just held me in his arms quietly. Silence was all I wanted, it was less painful that way. All that could be heard in the silent room were my sobs. How could he not be fed up with me when I myself was weary of all the sorrow dragging around my heart like a dead weight? However exasperated or weary he may have been, he never said anything that might hurt my feelings.

"Everything'll be fine once we leave," was the only thing he'd say, and the words turned into a mantra in the months following the miscarriage. I would agree and say after him, "Yes, once we leave, everything will be okay." We repeated and clung to those words like an invocation but our faith in them was quite different. There were days when I was wracked by doubt and the invocation vied against a nagging question: would everything really be 'fine' after I finished my studies and we left this hellhole? Or would I always be plagued by this constant feeling that I was falling over and over again into a dark and arid pit where not a drop of moisture was to be found besides my tears?

I am alone in the pit; Luay hasn't fallen into it with me, although he can see where I have landed. He can see with his own eyes that I am crouching at the bottom, he can tell how bad my fall was, and I watch him above ground trying to pull me out with his hand extended, but unable to do so. The pit is so deep no one can get down inside it. And it's so narrow, there's only room in it for my own sorrow. This is no fantasy, it is something real that I experience in a constantly recurring nightmare.

I see myself lying on the bed in a clean hospital room. The ceilings are high and white, like the walls. The doctor's coat and hijab are also white as are the uniforms and hijabs of the nurses standing around the bed. In the nightmare, I'm not a doctor but a patient. I feel as though I have rocks in my head. Their glances travel to the right of the bed; I turn with difficulty and see my swaddled baby lying in a crib with his eyes shut. His hands and feet twitch like a fledgling trying to fly. My heart flutters and soars toward him. I want to hold him in my arms and kiss him. I stretch out my hand but I can't reach. I tell them I'd like to hold him in my lap but I have no voice and they don't respond. The doctor smiles and she gestures to me to come closer. When I try to get up, everything spins around and around and my head starts pounding. The nurses are smiling but none of them move to try and help me. I sit up on the edge of the bed with my feet dangling in the air. They all disappear, the doctor as well as the nurses. Looking down, all I see is pitch-black darkness, and like a hot, rolling tear, I drop to the bottom of the pit. I hear myself screaming and crying as I fall. When I hit the bottom, I hear an explosion. I crouch down and hear a baby crying. I know it's my baby, even though I can't see him. My hand reaches out and I scream.

Then I wake up, soaked in tears and sweat, clenched up in a ball like a child crying for its mother, not like a mother crying over her child.

2

Holding me in his arms, I'm sure that Luay is thinking, "When are things going to go back to normal?"

He had hoped that I would get pregnant again and that it would somehow make up for our loss and erase our sorrow. That's what everyone trying to comfort us said: "Don't give up hope. Yalla, by the grace of God, you'll be rewarded with another baby." I didn't mind, even though the idea of being pregnant and studying at the same time seemed much harder than the first time around when I was able to do both without difficulty. My mother was always alluding to the subject, as was my mother-in-law. I guess they're entitled to want grandchildren. I would invariably respond by saying all in good time, but it seems as if a miracle might be needed. Since the miscarriage, we have only had sex three or four times, and not once did we finish. I really wanted to be aroused and the first time we did it, I responded to his kisses and caresses. But a strange mix of feelings I'd never had before began to stir inside me. When he took my nipple in his mouth and began nibbling and tugging on it, I burst into tears, and couldn't stop crying for an hour. He held me close in his arms and apologized, saying he'd probably gone too quickly. I told him I was sorry, and he was understanding and gentle. The second time, my body was completely unresponsive even though I felt I wanted it. Tears were the only thing my body produced, as if it were mourning what had been rent from it by force. I wondered whether the body had a will of its own and was able to refuse the dictates of the conscious mind? That is what I began to believe.

He tried to fool around a few more times after that but I always found excuses to put him off, saying I was tired or not in the mood. When he slept by my side and got aroused, he tried to guide my hand to his hard-on but I just wasn't interested. He got tired of my stalling tactics and repeated rejection, and gradually he stopped even trying to approach me. I'm not sure, but I suspect that he's just come to rely on himself in the bathroom every day. Maybe even in bed. I woke up one night as the bed was shaking but he must have stopped when he heard me moan in my sleep.

3

I feel terrible about erupting like a volcano in front of Youssef. I appreciate his generosity and kind-heartedness in hosting us all this time, and I will be indebted to him as long as I live. But I can't stand his pontificating, his oversimplifications, and a sort of bleeding heart that borders on naiveté. I want to be able to watch the news, comment, and express my opinion freely without getting into long drawn-out debates that make me uncomfortable because I have to respect my host and his viewpoints. I want to curse and criticize whomever and whatever I please, even if "that's not objective," as he keeps telling me. But I'm not in my own house, and I can't go back home because I don't have a home anymore. Of course, I could stay upstairs in our apartment and watch the news there. It's not like I watch a whole lot anyway, but it wouldn't be polite to use the house like a hotel and not keep him company when there is an opportunity to do so. Youssef welcomed us with open arms and wouldn't hear of us paying rent.

Once my tears had ebbed and my sorrow subsided, I wanted to ask Luay what Youssef had said after I'd left the room and how upset he was, but I could tell by the way he was breathing deeply that he had fallen asleep. He'd had a long and tiring day at work, as always, and that made me feel even more guilty. I vowed to apologize to Youssef before leaving for school the next day and to make him tabsi badhinjan, his favorite dish, as soon as I had the chance. He would forgive me, I was sure, he knew how much I loved and respected him, even if we disagreed strongly about the fate of our community and the intensifying sectarianism in the country. All of creation was close to his heart, and that included me.

Yes, I would apologize to him, even though I'm convinced that he's living in the past. Despite his forays into the present, he is still cloistered in his own circumscribed world. Even though he read widely and follows the news closely, he has no idea what I go through every day. Of course, he goes out to buy the papers and groceries, and to visit his friend once in a while, although his friend also lives in his own world, just like him. He spends most of his time at home, listening to old songs and reading, or sitting outside and taking care of his garden. The beautiful courtyard is like a desert island—it is completely cut off from the ocean of ugliness surrounding it. You can't even see the street when you're sitting there.

He doesn't have to deal with all the people I have to interact with on a daily basis. He doesn't hear the things I hear or see what I see every day. He can't imagine what it's like for a woman to be looked at the way they look at me. It feels as if they're looking through me, as if they're X-raying me to determine the extent of my disease, of my defilement, just because I'm not like them and don't belong with them. And it's not just men who look at me that way but also women; they stare and make me feel I'm a whore for not wearing a hijab. I catch my fellow classmates looking at me sideways and whispering among themselves. I know that's what they're talking about. I held out for two years, but then I caved in and started covering my head, using the scarf that I wear to church. I wear it everywhere now just so people stop looking at me in that way.

All I want is to live in a place where I'm like other people, where I can come and go as I please without anyone pointing at me or reminding me that I am different.

I was filling in a form once at a government office, and the guy processing my papers said, "Your father's name is George? That's a foreign name, isn't it?"

"No, it's not foreign, it's Iraqi," I told him.

"Oh, really? George isn't foreign? You know, like George Bush?"

"No, like George Wassouf. And George Qurdahi."

He stamped the form and handed it back to me, but I could feel his contempt. His eyes were filled with loathing as he asked petulantly, "Why don't you people go and find yourselves some good Arabic names? There's no shortage of names is there?"

I didn't say anything. There was no point in arguing with a despicable bigot. And that was neither the first nor the last time. When I told my father, he recounted a story about Abdel-Salam Arif, one of the presidents long before I was even born. In one of his speeches to a large crowd, he apparently said,

"No more Johnnys and Georges from now on. Only Hamads and Hmuds!" Abdel-Salam Arif was a lunatic, Father added. Once he was giving a speech and was so exasperated with their cheering that he blurted, "Stop so I can finish this shit!"

One time, I had taken a bag of klaicha to school with me and when I took them out to eat them before the lecture, one of the other students who knew I was a Christian expressed surprise. "You guys also eat klaicha?" he asked. I was so annoyed I couldn't hide it.

"Yes, we eat klaicha and we drink tea—and water—just like you do. What do you think we are, Martians?"

But the guy just kept on. "I've heard that when midnight strikes on New Year's Eve, your priests switch off the lights and tell every guy to turn around and kiss the girl next to him. Is that true?"

I picked up the cookies, my book bag, and my purse and stormed away. I never spoke to him again, and he hasn't apologized for his crassness to this day.

I roil with anger when I occasionally see posts on Facebook accusing Christians of collaborating and helping the occupation forces, just because some of them work with the American army. I write back furious responses reminding the other person that plenty of Muslims work for the occupation army, and that Iraqi politicians who welcomed the invasion and called for the Americans to intervene in the country, and then worked closely with the occupation authorities for many years, were all Muslims. My posts are full of exclamation points and question marks, and always formulated as questions. Hadn't the current ruling elite come in on the heels of the occupation? Hadn't all the religious and sectarian parties and groups cooperated with the occupiers? Weren't Iran, Turkey, and Saudi Arabia all supporting this or that group, while no one championed us Christians? I've unfriended several people who had allowed others to post vitriolic comments about Christians on their walls.

I was exhausted, because everything and everyone, with or without reason, reminded me that I was just a 'minority.' Things got so bad that I even stopped wearing the gold cross around my neck that my grandmother had given me on my First Communion. Before, I would tuck it under my clothes in order to avoid prying eyes. When the fine gold chain from which it hung broke, I didn't take it to the goldsmith to have it fixed. Instead I put it back in the small box it came in and carried it around in my purse like a lucky charm. Sometimes when I'm home, I take it out and press it to my lips, and I get tearful remembering my grandmother.

I want to live freely, and wear whatever I please around my neck, whatever length of dress I choose. Youssef cautioned me many a time that emigrating to countries where the majority of people are Christian is not without its own hardships and difficulties, and it wouldn't mean that I won't also feel like a minority there. He says I will face racism by virtue of being Arab. He speaks as if he'd been living abroad for years, even though he hasn't set foot outside the country for ages. And even when he did travel, it was only ever on short trips, as a member of official delegations to foreign countries. I'd tell him that I was ready to put up with and accept anything in exchange for living without car bombs, terror, and sectarianism.

"Alright, my dear, please yourself," he'd mutter back.

4

Youssef is always talking about how stable everything used to be, but I have no clear image of that word in my mind or my memory. The narrator of my past isn't stability but its very opposite—even going back to before the fall of the regime and the American invasion. When I recall my childhood, I don't see the types of scenes that are portrayed in films, at least in traditional 'happy' films: blowing out candles on a birthday cake, surrounded by loved ones singing happy birthday who then shower you with presents. Of course, we had celebrations and presents and there were the odd moments of happiness here and there, but to me, these are like tiny islands bobbing on a deep ocean of sorrow that has swallowed up my loved ones and taken them from me.

How can I forget the disappearance of Uncle Mukhlis, my amazingly tall uncle who spoiled me like no one else? Whenever he visited his greeting to me was always, "Hi there, my Maha! Shall we go flying, just like the birds?" Drawn in by his laughing eyes and mischievous dimples, I could never resist the fanciful offer. There were strings attached, however, and he was unrelenting about them: I had to kiss him four times and hug him very tight—"Tighter, tighter," he would say. I loved hugging him, his cologne smelled so good. Like fruit and the flavored gum I liked. Once all the kissing and hugging were done, his strong arms would gather me up and hold me aloft as we twirled around the courtyard, and Uncle Mukhlis would tell me that when I grew up I would sprout wings and be able to flit between the trees and land on their branches. Then, he would stand still and throw me up into the air, and catch me as I came down. I would squeal with a mixture of fear and delight and ask him to do it again. He always agreed and would throw me up in the air over and over again until my mother came out and said, "Enough, Mukhlis. Come on inside, the two of you."

Mukhlis was my only uncle. One day, he disappeared, and there were no more visits or aerial circling lessons.

"Where is Uncle Mukhlis?" I'd ask. "Isn't it time he came over?" and they would tell me that he had traveled somewhere far away and would be back soon.

After he disappeared, my mother became sad and would cry inconsolably. It was then that I learned a new word, which I'd hear the adults using when they spoke to each other and when neighbors and relatives came over. In between her tears, my mother would recount what had happened, and use the word *kidnapping*. And there was also *ransom*, which often went with it

"What does kidnapping mean?" I'd ask my mother but she'd shoo me away and say it was none of my business. "Go and play outside!" she'd exclaim.

Later I learned that kidnapping meant that someone you loved didn't come back because the bad men (whom I imagined looked like movie villains) took him somewhere far away and asked for huge sums of money in order to release him. I noticed the heated arguments and the phone calls and the hours of suspense. I would stand behind the living room door and eavesdrop on the adults going back and forth about the best course of action to follow. I found out that Father had managed to collect the sum required for the ransom and that the meeting with the kidnappers would take place behind the amusement park, on al-Qanat Highway. I was so happy that my uncle was coming back! He was sure to bring me lots of sweets, the way he always did when he visited.

When I asked my mother if he was coming over, she didn't yell at me. Instead, she replied, "God willing, Maha. He'll be back by the grace of the Almighty."

But only more sorrow followed. When Father came back from the much-anticipated meeting two days later, he wrapped his arms around her and uttered, "Mukhlis is gone." Just that one sentence. My mother screamed and wailed and slapped her head, beside herself with grief. She wept for weeks afterward.

The women of the family put on their mourning black and for three days the house was filled with visitors. Some of them were relatives whom I knew and recognized, but many were strangers. The men sat in the reception lounge and the women in the family room. I asked everyone about Uncle Mukhlis and all the answers I got were a variant on the statement that he'd gone somewhere far away. I knew that people who traveled came back, but this was a one-way journey, they said. The only thing that made it back was his smiling face in black and white inside a frame that my mother hugged to her chest as she wept. She eventually hung it up on the wall in the family room. The only cheer in all the misery came from the man my father hired to make coffee for the mourners during the three days of the aza mourning ceremony. The coffee man was extremely kind to me, he would come in early in the morning and set up his gear in the small alcove off the vestibule that led to the reception lounge. I would watch as he placed the coffee pot over the charcoal embers to boil the coffee. And I noticed how he'd slide his hand into a paper bag and pull out little green pods that he dropped into the coffee, keeping one for himself. When he popped it into his mouth, I wondered if he was going to chew it.

"Is it gum?" I asked.

"No, sweetie," he replied, laughing. "It's hayl. Would you like some?" I nodded and he gave me one. Holding it between my fingers, I examined the cardamom pod.

"So why do you put it in your mouth?"

"Because it sweetens the breath," he replied. I began chewing on it but the seeds were bitter on my tongue. I was going to give them back to the coffee man, but when I spat them out into my palm along with a thread of saliva, he gently wiped my hand and mouth with a tissue and told me to go and get a drink of water. My mouth was still bitter afterward. The disappearance of my uncle was the other seed of bitterness that was sown in that sad time—but it just grew and multiplied, and water was no remedy for it.

During the condolence period, my grandmother kept repeating between her tears that he had been kidnapped and killed because he was a Christian. When we talked about my uncle's disappearance a month ago, Youssef, as usual, provided a more 'objective' explanation. He said that Mukhlis had been kidnapped because he owned a clothing store and the kidnappers assumed his family would come up with the ransom money. He said abductions had become a scourge that affected everyone equally, irrespective of religion or denomination. Kidnappers preferred kidnapping people without tribal ties because they were afraid of retribution. It's strange that I don't remember Youssef being at the aza but he recalls the details well.

5

In the mid-nineties, when I was in elementary school, my father sank into depression and was laid up for many months. I would come home from school, which was close to our house, and find him sitting alone on a chair in our little garden. He'd sit there smoking one cigarette after the other staring into the void that now filled his days. I would greet him exuberantly and he would answer with a broad grin, a few endearments and a "Hello, there," after I had kissed his cheek, which was rough and prickly because he'd stopped shaving regularly. He wouldn't ask me much about my day and what we'd learned at school the way he used to. The Faith Campaign launched by Saddam had forced my father to close the bar that he owned with his business partner. Our primary source of income had dried up, the losses grew, and with them our worries, because my mother's salary as a secretary in a doctor's office wasn't sufficient to cover our expenses.

One day, I came home to find him standing outside the house next to a small pile of broken bricks, instructing two workmen with shovels in their hands. They had just demolished part of the exterior wall and were digging up a small patch of earth in a corner of the garden. "What's going on, Baba?" I asked. "What are the men doing?"

He told me they were building a little store where he would sell whatever he could to improve our situation. "I've got to keep you fed, girl," he said.

I had overheard my mother saying, "A store, why not? Better than sitting at home all day twiddling your thumbs."

At first, the news made me happy because it meant that I could have all the good stuff like candy and lollipops that my father would sell at the store. I'd be able to show off in front of my friends and the girls next door. While it was true that I was able to have whatever I wanted for free, I paid a terrible price for it. The structure took up one-third of our small garden, and with all the boxes and cartons of merchandise piled up outside, there was almost no room left to play. My little sister, Shadha, and I no longer had a garden in which to run around and be free as the birds.

As it turned out, the store wasn't much help in alleviating Father's despondency. The sighs of weariness, the cigarette puffing, the head hung low, and all the other signs of depression were back. The only thing that cheered him up and helped smooth the furrow of his brow was the fact that I was smart and excelled in school. He smiled when one day I used the word 'median.' I had heard the adults using it in conversation and had seized on it even though it was beyond my years. "Well, look at that! And you're just in elementary school!" he said, giving me a kiss.

6

I'm trying to remember a time when I haven't felt alienated, smothered, or, as now, destitute. To me, our exodus from the house in al-Dawra didn't take place all at once in the summer of 2007. Rather, it was one of an unbroken sequence of events that spanned many years. It's as if chunks of me were lopped off or stolen bit by bit, until nothing was left. First, they kidnapped my uncle and killed him. Even though he didn't live with us under the same roof, he was, for me, such an intimate part of the family that his absence left a gaping hole in our house. After my uncle's abduction, my father's eyes lost their sparkle and our little garden was ripped up for the sake of the store. And that wasn't the end of it. Perhaps Youssef was right on one count, when he said that nothing prior to 2003 bore any resemblance to the savagery that came afterward.

All of us rejoiced at the fall of Saddam, especially Father, even though he didn't trust the Americans or their motives. But he was taken in, like so many others, and really believed it when they said on the news that Iraq was destined to become another Hong Kong, never imagining that it would end up looking far more like Somalia. But he made a smart move: two months after the fall of the regime, he turned the corner store into a shop that sold satellite dishes. They'd been banned before the occupation and now demand for them skyrocketed. Everybody, including us, hurried to buy one and get a vista on the outside world that we'd been deprived of for so many years.

Financially, our situation improved to the point that Father began looking into shutting down the corner store and opening a bar with a new business partner, but as his plan matured and he continued to scout for a suitable location, the security situation deteriorated rapidly. Explosions and car bombs blasted through the air and the language of death proliferated, obliterating the peace we thought would be ours. Father's potential partner backed out because he didn't think the situation bode well for a bar or any other kind of business venture. Father was devastated—a year or so after the Americans' arrival, demand for satellite dishes dwindled and the profits dried up.

Early on, this language of death had been aimed at those who worked with the Americans and cooperated with them or with the new government. With time, however, the deadly messages proliferated, going to select recipients and destinations, and the once verbal onslaught became physical, engulfing us in a blaze of fire and destruction we could never have imagined. For years, the voice of the preacher had reverberated from the mosque loudspeaker urging the faithful to godliness and piety and against irreligion. I hadn't paid it much heed because I didn't feel targeted by his discourse; the messages hadn't seemed aimed at me, as a Christian. But in the chaos that resulted from the occupation, what we had deemed to be a temporary clamor grew shrill. Unfamiliar words like 'dhimmi'—protected citizen—and 'jizya'—poll tax—began circulating. Words which Hatam al-Razzaq, the imam of al-Noor Mosque in our neighborhood, repeated loudly after conferring on himself the title of 'amir' in 2007. He began to rant into the loudspeakers, calling for so-called dhimmis to pay a monthly jizya of $25,000 or else openly convert to Islam at the mosque. Whenever he heard him ranting like that, Father would slap his hand across his forehead.

"That's all we need!" he'd exclaim. "What hole did this guy crawl out of? Where are we supposed to get five stacks? Is this what we have come to, dhimmis?" But my mother clung to hope, telling him—and herself—that the preacher was just a lunatic. "He'll just rave and rant like that for a few days and then he'll be gone."

The lunatic went on, however, repeating the same thing over and over again, in increasingly more shrill and strident tones. Had it just been him, it wouldn't have been that bad. He would eventually have grown tired and given up, but there were plenty of people who listened to him and did his bidding.

First, there were verbal threats, and later handwritten messages began arriving at the door of Christian homes. To remain in the neighborhood, the one-week ultimatum stipulated, you either converted or paid the jizya. My father tore up the first such letter and didn't tell my mother about it. He tried to find out if there was any way to get to the amir or his representatives and work out a deal, or pay them off somehow, but he made no headway. At the end of the week's notice, another letter arrived, with the same ultimatum signed by a group calling itself Jaysh Muhammad. After that, the messages became more eloquent, coming in the form of bullets and hand grenades. Then, they burned down the Assyrian church and attacked St. John the Baptist, the church we attended on Sundays, vandalizing the cross atop its dome.

Then one night, shots were fired through our kitchen window and we found the words 'infidels' scrawled in red paint across the front door. We filed complaints with the police department and the church made appeals to the government on our behalf, to no avail.

Father closed down the store and we packed what we could and fled to my uncle's house in al-Baladiyat. The reception room in their house turned into a small encampment for us and all our bags and possessions. We were there for four months. Shadha had to move to a new school, and the situation in al-Dawra went from bad to worse: there were more and more attacks on churches, bomb blasts, mortar attacks, and two priests were abducted. Going back there was out of the question and many Christians left, fleeing to Syria and Jordan. A number of my mother's relatives went to Ainkawa in the north, and they urged us to follow suit because the area was peaceful. We heard that we might be able to apply for religious asylum through the UN or NGOs that had begun to operate there.

Father went ahead so as to get the lay of the land. He rented a small apartment and came back to fetch us. He gave our trusted neighbor, Abu Muhammad, the keys to our house and to the store and asked him to sell the remaining furniture and find a renter or buyer for the house. Father said that Abu Muhammad apologized as he embraced him emotionally.

"Nonsense!" Father told him. "It's not your fault!"

"We didn't look out for you, Abu Maha. You were entrusted to our care and we didn't protect you."

"All of us are guilty, Abu Muhammad. None of us looked out for Iraq," Father replied.

I was supposed to return to Baghdad at the end of the summer in order to complete the three remaining years I had at medical school, or else I would have to start all over again when I went abroad. I had heard that if I completed my degree, it would be easier to have it recognized after. I'd only need to study for another couple of years elsewhere, rather than go back to square one. My father supported my plan and he accompanied me to Baghdad at the beginning of my fourth year, and we stayed with my uncle once again. He tried to liquidate our house in al-Dawra once more, but nobody wanted to buy there, so he closed it up and returned to Ainkawa. He looked for work, to no avail, but fortunately my mother found a job at a women's clothing store and they registered my sister, Shadha, at the local school. They lived on my mother's wages and on the money my aunt sent them from Canada every month.

7

My uncle and his family welcomed me like a daughter. Even though my parents were far away and I missed them, a mattress on the floor in my uncle's reception lounge was better than the tiny room in Ainkawa. I spent most of my time studying, anyhow. Aside from classes, I only went out to go to the Church of the Martyr Mar Bathyoun on Sundays or to attend a lecture or film organized by the church as part of a series held on the first Friday of every month to educate the congregation about Christian thought. The first lecture I attended was in honor of the church's eponymous saint and I found his life story and all its ramifications fascinating. He was born to a Zoroastrian family in the lower Zab region of northern Iraq but converted to Christianity. Then he became an ascetic and lived a life of austerity and devotion based on the teachings of the Bible. People would seek him out to pray over and cure the sick. Bathyoun spread the Christian message without fear of retribution from the Zoroastrians. During the winters, he came down from the mountains and carried his message to the south. Because he got so many of the notables of the society at the time to convert, the Zoroastrian chief judge ordered Bathyoun to be brought to him shackled. He was charged with witchcraft and thrown into prison but during the night, his shackles fell away and he walked out of the jail, praising the Lord. The other inmates watched in amazement as the prison doors opened wide and their own shackles also fell away miraculously.

"Your God, O Bathyoun," they cried out in unison, "is mighty and majestic. Blessed are those that lean on Him."

The ruler ordered him to be thrown into the river and left to drown, but the waters stopped flowing and only resumed their course once he was pulled out by royal decree. The ruler cried out in anger and swore on the life of Yazdegurd the Great that Bathyoun would be burned alive, but when they placed him in the furnace, the fire died down. Bathyoun was brought before the council of elders who sentenced him to what was known as the 'nine deaths'—a gradual dismemberment of his body over a period of six days. When he was taken to the torture chamber, he repeated the Lord's words from the Gospel of Matthew:

And fear not them which kill the body, but are not able to kill the soul: but rather fear him which is able to destroy both soul and body in hell.

The lectures would usually conclude with a short group discussion and then we all trooped out to the courtyard for refreshments and pastries. I will always remember that lecture because it brought Luay into my life. He was a regular at church and at the monthly gatherings. Our eyes met several times and then he smiled at me; a smile that felt calming as my head thronged with all the details of Bathyoun's torture and suffering. At the next lecture, he made sure to sit by me, and at the end of the discussion he asked me where I was from. I told him the story of my family's escape from Baghdad and that I had remained in the city to finish my studies. I came across him a week later wandering around the campus of the medical school and he flashed me that same smile when he saw me. He expressed his gladness at running into me and told me he was looking for one of his old friends from high school. He admitted later on that the "running into me" had been orchestrated and that he had concocted the story of his high school friend so that we could meet far from the church and watchful eyes. He asked if I'd like to go and get a fresh juice with him and we spent two lovely hours that flew by as we chatted. We exchanged cell phone numbers before parting.

He was four years older than me, tall and handsome, and he wore his soft black hair short. His inky eyes lit up every time he laughed. He had studied English in the language department at Baghdad University, and during his last year there had worked at Qasr Marjan, the hotel that his uncle owned. After graduating, he was promoted to administrative manager with a good salary.

At first, we talked on the phone, and then we started meeting once a week. We'd hang out, talk and laugh about things. He made me feel good, I felt comfortable and relaxed around him. When he broached the subject of marriage about six months later, I was ecstatic. He traveled to Ainkawa to meet my parents, and they were both impressed. They liked him as a person, they approved of his values, and they agreed to our getting married as long as I completed my studies—which was exactly what I wanted. He didn't try to kiss me until after we were engaged. I was nervous when he did, and didn't know what to do when his tongue touched my lips and then slipped inside my mouth. He was nervous too. At first, our kisses were awkward but they soon settled into a lovely rhythm.

8

The marriage ceremony was held at Mar Bathyoun Church where we met, and it was followed by a modest reception in the hall of the hotel that Luay managed. My parents came in from Ainkawa and Luay made the necessary arrangements for them to stay at the hotel at a very reduced rate. Watching me cut the five-tiered wedding cake in my white gown, my mother cried tears of joy. Youssef came and he, too, congratulated us. Because of my classes and Luay's job, we couldn't take time off to go away, so three nights at the Hamra Hotel was our honeymoon. Afterward, we moved into a room that Luay had furnished with a new bedroom set on the second floor of his parents' house in Zayyouna.

About five months later, Luay suggested we move into my parents' house in al-Dawra since the situation there had improved considerably after the forces of the Awakening Movement had taken control of the area. The house lay empty, there were no renters and my parents had no intention of returning. To begin with, I was hesitant because I was afraid of what might happen, but Luay reassured me, saying the area had been secured and Christian families had begun to return to the neighborhood.

Even though I wasn't entirely convinced, I finally agreed to this after watching a TV story about the reopening of our church. The vandalized cross had been restored to its place on the cupola, and the footage showed some Muslims from the neighborhood sitting side by side with the remaining members of the Christian community at a church service. I was moved when I saw some of them looking straight at the camera and urging their 'Christian brethren,' as they called us, to return to their homes because the area was now safe.

"Don't leave your homes to strangers, come back and live among us; you'll be respected and supported. We are one family." The man who spoke looked directly into the camera as he distributed sweets in the church courtyard. His words went straight to my heart and I choked up with tears. I knew that we would be more comfortable if we had our own place and my parents agreed to the idea, especially my mother who wasn't in favor of my living with my in-laws too long, even though they were extremely nice and I didn't have a single complaint about them.

"Go on, sweetheart. You'll feel more comfortable there. It'll do you good," she kept telling me.

My father had been in touch with our neighbor, Abu Muhammad, and he too had confirmed that things had gotten much better since the situation had stabilized. Luay paid for a few repairs as well as the repainting of the interior, and he hired someone to move in the bedroom set he had purchased when we got married. I insisted that we sleep in my old room. Even though my parents' bedroom was more spacious, I couldn't stand the idea of sleeping there—it felt too embarrassing.

The first few days back at our house I had very mixed and confused feelings. I wasn't used to being there without my parents, and it was strange sleeping under that roof with my husband, even though I loved him and we were making a fresh start on our own. There were times I felt really sad and I would dream of Uncle Mukhlis whose ghostly shadow still inhabited the garden. The emptiness I felt and my feelings of loneliness didn't abate until the baby started moving inside me a year and a half later.

We had agreed to postpone having children until I'd finished my studies, and I was careful about us avoiding the days when I might get pregnant. Despite my calculations, I missed a period and all the early signs of pregnancy appeared. Luay thought I'd be upset because I was so determined not to let anything interfere with my studies, but I was more thrilled by the news than he was and felt confident that I would be able to manage my time. The baby was due at the beginning of summer according to the doctor, a time when I had no exams or lectures to attend. My mother-in-law said she would be happy to come and live with us for the first few months and look after the baby when I had to go to class. Luay fixed up Shadha's bedroom for the baby boy we were expecting according to the ultrasound, and we agreed to name him Bashar. Luay's mother bought the crib and a layette, and put them in the baby's room.

9

Everything was ready for the baby's arrival, from soft sheets to loving arms. He moved constantly and seemed in a hurry to leave his little chamber in my body and join the rest of the world. But he never made it to his room and his crib remained empty. Not because I made a mistake, or because I didn't take care of the body of which he was a part. I followed my doctor's instructions meticulously, and 'nothing but the best' was my approach to the pregnancy. But his fate was sealed by perfect strangers, by people who had nothing to do either with him or with us. There is no answer or explanation for why the end arrives too early—it's always stark and distressing. But how much more terrible is it when a life ends before it has even begun? How awful is it when death precedes birth itself?

No one knows where the two booby-trapped cars came from that night or how they managed to steal into the neighborhood, but it was all too clear that our street was targeted because most of the residents were Christians. There were no targets of strategic value such as a police station or government office. The area had been quiet and stable for months, with fighters from the Sahwa militia controlling the streets and major access points. They were paid a monthly wage in exchange for which they committed to point the barrels of their guns in the right direction, namely against al-Qaeda and other terrorists rather than training them on us Christians, or on the Americans and the Shiites.

The two cars, one of which was parked directly in front of our house, exploded shortly after four o'clock that morning, destroying a large chunk of the garden wall and shattering the windows. Pieces of shrapnel flew in every direction, landing on the roof and in the yard, and some of them found their way into our bedroom. Luckily, we had placed the bed away from the window and the broken glass cascaded onto the ground. The only thing I remember is hearing the explosion and screaming. I knew instantaneously that I would lose Bashar. I shook like a tree in a deathly storm. I felt that death itself was moving through me looking for my son to strangle in my womb. Luay wrapped his arms around me and tried to calm me. "It's okay, don't be scared," he kept repeating. "I'm right here, it's alright." I felt some wetness on the sheets and thought I must have lost control of my bladder from fear, but I quickly realized I was bleeding. I don't remember what happened after that. Luay told me afterward that I screamed like a madwoman for over half a minute and then fainted. When we got to the hospital, only one heart was beating inside my body instead of two.

Bashar was the fruit that was plucked by fear before it had ripened on the branch. Why did he have to fall to the ground without anyone catching him? Just like that, from the womb to the grave, without even passing through the cradle, without nursing at the breasts that were readying for him, without wearing the beautiful clothes we had bought him, or sleeping in the room that awaited him.

10

When I opened my eyes, my mother was sitting by my side, holding my hand. She kissed me and tried to comfort me. "The Lord giveth and the Lord taketh away. The most important thing is that you're safe," she said. Then the face of the doctor wearing a scarf appeared along with those of the nurses. Luay came in and kissed me on the forehead, and then my father followed. There were so many faces, faces that made me feel besieged as they stared at me and repeated the same stupid things. My parents and sister had hurried to Baghdad from Ainkawa to be near me, but Father and Shadha had to leave after three days so that Shadha wouldn't miss school.

I swore then and there that I would never again set foot in al-Dawra or return to that benighted house. When I was released from the hospital, we went back to the room we had lived in at Luay's parents. My mother stayed on in Baghdad to take care of me as I convalesced and Youssef heard about what happened from her. He called to ask how I was doing and to get my phone number because he wanted to talk to me. He was very kind and apologized for not coming to see me at the hospital but he'd only found out after the fact.

When my mother visited him before returning to Ainkawa and went into some detail about what had happened, he offered to have us move into the second floor of his house; he had turned it into a separate apartment in 1991 and it had been unoccupied for the last several months. She went and saw for herself that there was a spacious bedroom, a bathroom, and a kitchen and he assured her that we could feel at home and no one would bother us. The apartment had a separate entrance with its own outdoor staircase and we could come and go as we pleased.

I didn't hesitate for long because even though my husband's parents were kind to a fault I felt suffocated by the constant stream of visitors and really wanted a place where I could be alone and quiet. Luay got excited about it after we went to visit the apartment in Youssef's house, especially as it was close to his job and he could walk to work. Youssef flatly refused to discuss the rent with us or accept any kind of deposit. "Later, later," he kept saying. "Allah karim, God is generous."

He never accepted payment of any kind, even when Luay left money in an envelope for him. He told me that if I occasionally cooked him something, it would be worth far more to him than any rent we might pay. And that is what I did, in addition to helping out around the house. Luay, for his part, bought most of the fruit and also shopped for groceries.

11

The truth is I never really came back from the hospital. That is what my mother said. I just wasn't the same Maha anymore. A part of me had died and been buried with the baby. Even though I didn't wear black, my heart was shrouded in mourning and two dark clouds were lodged behind my eyes, ready to burst at any moment. Every day was like running the long and arduous laps of a marathon against my will. I did what was required as a student, going to lectures and studying. I looked after Luay and tried to be nice to him.

Even though he and I shared a bed, my body was in another world; it was as if it were visiting the part of me that had died—to grieve over it, so that I too could begin to grieve. Whenever Luay tried to approach me playfully, I would shrink away like a petrified flower. I realized how much I had changed and admitted as much.

"Your blossom has wilted," I told him when he took me in his arms, whispering, as he always did, that I was his flower.

He would comfort me, as he kissed my forehead, and say, "My flower doesn't wilt. It's just bruised."

12

I became hypersensitive to noise after the bombing incident and the slightest sound would startle me. I felt better after we moved to the apartment in Youssef's house because it was quiet there, and once my mother had left, I really enjoyed the quietness. My mother felt that I had made a good recovery, at least physically, and that she could go back to Ainkawa to her job and the rest of our family. Unlike my in-laws' place, Youssef's house was on a quiet side street that had little or no traffic since one of its exits was blocked by large concrete barriers that only allowed pedestrians through. Other than for the maqams which Youssef listened to occasionally, and the sound of the door to the backyard opening and clos- ing, I rarely heard any noise coming from downstairs when I was home from school. Occasionally, the faint sound of the satellite stations that Youssef watched drifted upstairs and punctured the solitude of my evenings, and I would some- times hear him talking back and arguing with whatever the newscasters were saying, but none of this bothered me. I had gotten used to the earplugs that the doctor had given me when I was having trouble sleeping at the beginning, and I used them a lot because I craved silence. I even wore them on my way to and from school to mute the din of cars and people. I almost died once when I was crossing the road engrossed in my thoughts. I heard what sounded like a loud squeak and looked up to see a woman on the sidewalk with her hand across her mouth and a man next to her raising his hand in the air as he looked at me. When I turned around to look behind me, I saw a white car not more than a meter from where I stood. The furious driver leaned out of the window and began shouting.

"Hey, what do you think you're doing walking in the middle of the street? Are you blind? What are sidewalks for?"

His lips looked like they were slapping against each other as he screamed.

I felt terrible and apologized repeatedly, gesturing with my hands, but the words must have been inaudible; I could tell neither he nor anyone else heard them. As he drove off, he twirled his index finger back and forth on his temple in a gesture telling me I was crazy.

13

My spirit found solace in another world in which I looked onto the torment of the saints and the agony of the Virgin Mary and her son. As soon as I was done with the reading I had to do for school, I would turn to the Bible which my grandmother, Nana, had given me, and to a couple of books I'd found in Hinna's room. I had gone in to clean the room one day because it had become so dusty and I found *Treasure of Worship* and the *Marian Month* there. I'd always loved Jesus and Mary, ever since I was little, but after the incident, I felt that I had discovered a deeper dimension to the Virgin; I now understood what she represented for those in distress.

I became obsessed with Fairouz's religious repertoire, especially the Easter hymns. I would listen to her on my headphones or turn up the volume really loud and let her chants fill the house, after I had to stop using the earplugs when they started to cause an allergic reaction and became painful from overuse. I would close my eyes and visualize Fairouz's voice as a flight of angels picking up the shreds of my heart and stitching them together. They would gather me up and take me with them to the eternal garden of sorrows. I didn't feel the need to say anything to anyone, not even to myself—Fairuz voiced all my pain and conveyed perfectly how my heart was encased in a wreath of thorns, along with everything else.

> I am the mother of sorrows, with no one to console her,
> May the death of your son be a life for those who seek it,
> The mother of Jesus wept, and her onlookers wept.
> I pity a nation that kills its shepherd
> Doves cry over the scattering of its people
> Come to Mary, his mother, let us console her.

> O beloved, O beloved, what has become of you?
> He who sees you cannot but grieve for you, the Redeemer,
> O beloved, with what sins did the Just one burden his children?
> Upon you they inflicted wounds that cannot heal,
> That night, when God the savior prostrated in the grove, praying,
> All of creation prayed for the one who enriched us with prayer,
> The olive trees weep, and lips call out to him,
> "O my beloved, whither do you go? Is faithfulness forever lost?"
> . . .
> Speak to me, speak to me, O beloved son!
> How can I see you thus and not weep for you?
> Your wounds sear my entrails,
> Your agony pierces my heart,

What life for you mother, after your death, O my
son?

And from death's cradle, I would hear Bashar calling out:

O Mary, my mother, your keening my tears has
multiplied.
Have mercy and cease! Leave me, go back.
O Father, why do you forsake me in my pain?
My moans are suffocating me, my ribs are rent apart.

Luay was patient and devoted but his patience gave out
one evening when he came back and found me listening to
those chants with my eyes closed. He too enjoyed them from
time to time, and especially on the Feast of the Resurrection—
Easter—but not every single solitary day, as he put it.
"Come on, honey," he muttered. "Enough already. . . .
Every day has become Good Friday!"
He couldn't understand how I could wallow in such grief.
Nor why—it's not as if we'd lost the baby after he was born
or that I couldn't get pregnant again. That's what he told my
mother. I don't know why he didn't speak to me directly. It
was his son, his own flesh and blood, too. More than once,
he urged me to see a psychiatrist, but I wouldn't hear of it. I
hadn't gone crazy, I told him.
I did some Googling and found several sites which
said that depression after a miscarriage might last as long
as three years and not resolve even after a successful pregnancy. When I sent him the links, he apologized for being
hard on me, and I thought he'd finally understood, but not
a month passed before he started again, reminding me that
even Christ's anguish came to an end and that Good Friday
was followed by Holy Saturday, after which there was Easter
Sunday. "You're locking yourself up inside the Good Friday
part," he said.

The only hymns I'd listen to were *Mother of Sorrows*, *Alas My Beloved*, and *Mary Is Risen*, and as soon as they'd finish, I would go back to the beginning of the CD. "Why not let Fairuz also bring you her tidings of hope and redemption?" he asked.

I had tried to listen to some of the other Easter canticles, but I didn't like them as much as the songs of sorrow. They didn't mean anything to me.

> O, Virgin who is pure, rejoice, I say also rejoice
> For your only son rose from the grave on the third day
> O New Jerusalem, light up for the Lord's glory unfolding
> Rejoice now and celebrate O Jerusalem
> And you, pure Mother of God,
> Be gladdened by the resurrection of your son
> Christ has risen from the dead and has stamped on death with death
> This is the day the Lord has given us to rejoice and celebrate.

The Son of God rose from the dead every year, but the son of man, my son, went to his death before even being born and he would never rise again. My womb was a tomb and my body its graveyard—one that I could visit at any time without going anywhere.

14

I began to visit the garden of sorrows, where Jesus prayed for the last time with his disciples, on a regular basis. I would kneel down every Friday evening to pray for an hour and read Christ's message to me in the *Treasury of Worship*. I would accompany him in the agony that he suffered in Gethsemane as he tried to soften the bitter blow of his disciples forsaking him when they were unable to stay awake with him even for one hour.

I now believe what my grandmother used to tell me when I was little. She said that olives had been a sweet fruit and that they only turned bitter the night Jesus cried alone in Gethsemane and the olive tree drank in his tears. As a child, I tried to imagine how bitterness came to be lodged in the olive tree that had imbibed Jesus's grief. How had olives in the rest of the world become bitter? Did the tree tell the other trees in Gethsemane of Christ's pain? Had its branches breathed out his tears in the form of dew? Did the roots of the tree whisper to those of its neighbors? And how had the news spread throughout the olive groves of the earth?

15

I'm carrying my infant, he is crying from thirst. All around us is the desert. There's just one cloud above our heads, it's moving with the wind, and a voice from the sky says, *Run after the cloud! Soon, it will burst and release its waters. Run, run that your son may drink!* And I run, naked and barefoot, but the cloud doesn't stop, and it doesn't burst. I run and run, panting, as my child cries. The cloud moves faster and I cannot keep up with it. It disappears on the horizon. I shush my baby and try to give him my tears to drink but all he does is cry. I wake up crying and my baby isn't there.

I'd wake up from these nightmares wet with tears, climb out of bed and quietly go down the stairs to Hinna's room. There I felt calm. I'd lie down on her bed and go to sleep. One day, Youssef came in, but as soon as he saw me he left the room. He must have heard me coming down. He never asked me why I had been sleeping there or said anything about it afterward.

16

Facebook became my window on the world, and I'd log in to get news of my sister, Shadha, and of our relatives in the Iraqi diaspora. I'd look at whatever new photos they had posted of special celebrations or visits they had organized, and would read their comments. I'd look for Shadha online and would chat with her there or through Skype whenever she was at the internet café close to where they lived because they didn't have internet at home. I'd ask her about school, about our parents, and about Ainkawa. I knew what was going on in a general sort of way because my mother called me regularly, but I wanted another version than the official family news that my mother always gave, saying everything was going well, there were no explosions or car bombs, and no power cuts. Everything was quiet, Mama would say, they were safe and just waiting for our emigration papers to come through. Then my father would get on briefly, he'd ask after Luay and tell me to convey his greetings to him and to Youssef.

The news according to Shadha was more substantial. I missed her and felt that she needed me. Shadha wasn't happy the first year they were in Ainkawa. She had a very hard time at school with her new teacher. Her grades dropped and she was no longer the outstanding student she had been in Baghdad. She complained about being lonely, she didn't have any real friends, and the only friend she had made that first summer had left for Sweden after her own family's emigration request had been approved. She said the atmosphere at home was depressing, that she was bored and felt suffocated because the three of them shared a bedroom. Father insisted on watching satellite TV all day, only the news mind you, even though it was always the same news, as Shadha said. He'd smoke and say very little except to reprimand her when she stayed out late at the internet café. The last time she and I spoke, she told me that our mother had had an argument with a Christian woman from Ainkawa who was complaining that the arrival of all the Baghdad Christians in their midst had caused rent inflation—they competed with locals over everything, down to the air they breathed!

"Even Christians are prejudiced," Shadha protested. She had to be patient, I said. Everything would be fine once we got to Canada. There, she would have a room of her own and a lot more freedom.

I got a request on Facebook from my friend, Israa, with whom I was happy to reconnect. She had dropped out of school two years earlier and married a relative of hers from Australia who had come back to the old country to find himself a bride after divorcing his Australian wife. She'd moved to Sydney without bothering to finish her degree because Australia didn't recognize credits earned in Iraq. She'd had to go back to square one and start from scratch.

I also found a Facebook group called Beautiful Iraq whose members exchanged photographs and songs from what they referred to as the good old days. There were rare and beautiful photos and the comments made by the members of the group reminded me of Youssef's accounts of the past and his lament over its ruination. That past where everything was wonderful and pristine. The strange thing was that for these people the past didn't begin or end in the same place. Some of them considered the Baath Party's coming to power and the brutal way Abdel-Karim Qasim was put to death as the end of the 'good' times. Others felt Saddam's accession to the presidency in 1979 was the beginning of the end. The good times stretched to 1991 for yet others who regarded the sanctions as the turning point for Iraq, and then there were some who considered the 2003 invasion the end. Most were nostalgic about the time of the monarchy and they posted photographs of the former royal family, the subtext being that their brutal execution in the military coup was the beginning of the descent into the abyss. Whenever I read these jeremiads, I'd wonder about the time of the monarchy: hadn't Assyrians been killed even during those halcyon days of royal rule? Hadn't Iraqi Jews effectively been expelled from their country overnight after being collectively dispossessed? Hadn't poverty been widespread? And the regimes that followed—weren't they soaked in the blood of the Kurds and the Shiites who were slaughtered and thrown into mass graves?

Beginnings and endings were all jumbled up. As they each cried over their own Iraq, I felt that I had no happy time to look back on. I looked at those pictures and the comments accompanying them and concluded that my halcyon days were yet to come. Maybe they would happen over there, in Canada, far from death, far from car bombs, far from all the hatred coursing through people's veins. We'd leave them the country so that they could torch it and desecrate its remains; they would shed bitter tears over what had once been only after it was too late.

17

Luay woke me with a kiss on the forehead before leaving for work. I asked him about Youssef and what had transpired the previous night. He said naturally, Youssef was upset, but he wasn't angry. I told Luay I was sorry about what had happened and he kissed me once again, this time on the cheek.

"It's okay," he said, "but make sure you apologize to him. I must get going."

We agreed to meet at home that evening so that we could go to church together, like we did every Sunday. I reminded him that it was the anniversary of Hinna's death.

I washed my face, got dressed quickly and went downstairs to apologize to Youssef before leaving for school. Even though his car was parked outside, he seemed to have gone out. I waited half an hour but had to leave after that. I almost called him but decided it would be best to apologize to him in person.

I wasn't able to focus on the dissection lecture and kept thinking back to what had happened the previous evening. I felt really bad: I loved Youssef and respected him, but I just didn't see the world the way he did. He didn't know what it was not to have one's own home and to feel preyed upon or threatened by potential predators. He didn't know, and would never know, what it was like for a woman to lose a baby. He didn't get it that the Muslims didn't want us in their midst and that they were treating us like intruders. How strange it was that he watched all these cable news shows and heard all the things they said yet insisted that it was all "merely a passing cloud."

The professor was talking about growing tissue and cell cultures in laboratory settings, citing examples that showed the incredible advances that had been made in recent decades. Years earlier, I would have been excited to learn more about the human body. I considered the human form to be exquisitely complex and felt glad that we were also blessed with a mind to understand it and protect the life that God had infused it with. It made me proud that I was going to be a doctor. All these new discoveries still impress me, but my enthusiasm has been replaced by feelings of nihilism. We spend long years in lecture halls and laboratories, and we wade through books to learn all the intricate details that other people have gathered over hundreds of years about how to care for the body and spare it suffering and death. But then others who are illiterate bigots come along and rip a body to pieces at the flick of a switch or by pressing a trigger. Blood everywhere, and the country becomes one massive dissection lab, but now instead of the dead, they experiment on the living. Deathology is the new science.

During moments of absolute despair, I would seek refuge in Jesus, and ask for his forgiveness. You commanded us to love our enemies, I'd pray silently, but I can't. I cannot love them. I don't understand them and I cannot curb the hatred and the revulsion I feel toward them. Especially when I see pictures of those enraged turban heads ranting on the satellite channels, their eyebrows bristling with anger and their hearts filled with rage. When I saw one of their faces leap out from a poster on my way home from school,

I couldn't help thinking that such hearts knew neither love nor mercy. We used to rail against the pictures of Saddam everywhere, and now posters of these men proliferated like amoeba. It was as if the same polluted material had been cloned and implanted anew.

The trip home was slow and it took twice as long as usual because there were new checkpoints due to a heightened security alert. The cars crawled along like exhausted tortoises. I was tired of the depressing grayness that had enveloped Baghdad. I wanted to live in a city with clean, tree-lined streets where the traffic flowed. A city that breathed, whose inhabitants could inhale the energy of life in public parks that weren't suffocating in a concrete jungle overflowing with garbage. My cell phone was in my purse, and my earplugs in my ears, and I didn't hear the phone ring when Luay called. I called him back when I got home. He said he would be getting to church a little late because a large delegation had just arrived at the hotel and he couldn't leave work at the usual time. I pleaded with him not to be too late because it was an important day for Youssef and suggested that he get in touch with him to let him know. He asked whether I had apologized to him. I told him Youssef wasn't home, even though his car was here. Most likely, he had gone to the church on foot.

The Eucharist

1

When Jesus came into the coasts of Caesarea Philippi, he asked his disciples, saying, "Whom do men say that I, the Son of Man, am?" And they said, "Some say that thou art John the Baptist; some, Elias; and others, Jeremias, or one of the prophets." He saith unto them, "But whom say ye that I am?" And Simon Peter answered and said, "Thou art the Christ, the son of the living God." And Jesus answered and said unto him, "Blessed art thou, Simon son of Jonah, for flesh and blood hath not revealed it unto thee but my Father which is in heaven. And I say unto thee, That thou art Peter, and upon this rock I will build my church; and the gates of hell shall not prevail against it."

Matthew, 16:13–18

Father Tha'ir had read the passage in his melodious voice and after he'd finished, he'd lifted the Bible from the wooden stand it rested on and held it up to expose its red velvet cover, its gold leaf-edged pages and the cross embossed in the center. He brought the book to his lips, raised it to his forehead, then closed it and placed it back on the stand. "O loved ones," he said, addressing the congregation, "let us pray for peace, that it may envelop our beloved land and bless us. Let us ask Almighty God for the successful formation of a new government which will protect us and watch over us. Say with me, '*Our Father who art in Heaven . . . .*'"

The congregation rose to intone the Lord's Prayer. As their voices rang out across the church with *"Give us this day our daily bread,"* the sound of gunfire drowned out the words. There was a momentary hesitation, a murmur rippled through the pews, but the recitation went on for the most part—people had grown used to the sounds of gunfire and explosions in recent years. Father Tha'ir reassured his flock.

"It's alright," he said, "let's go on."

But the gunfire didn't die down, it grew louder and more intense and sounded as if it were just outside the church door. People began turning around to look toward the door and a hubbub broke out. Speaking into the microphone, Father Tha'ir asked the young men standing by the entrance to lock the church door, and children began to cry. Then the entire building shook under the impact of a terrible explosion. Father Waseem, standing to the left of the altar, gestured to the congregation to run and hide in the sacristy, off to the side of the altar. A group of worshippers hurtled forward, but others remained frozen in place, as if the sound of the bullets outside had turned them to stone. Another part of the congregation headed for the side doors, which were normally kept closed because they led to the cemetery on either side of the church.

Youssef hesitated and remained standing in the pew; he wasn't sure what to do. He glimpsed Maha running toward the altar on the far left side. He almost went after her and he called her name twice but there was no way that she could've heard him—the three wooden panels of the entrance door had been blown off their hinges and men with automatic rifles burst into the church firing in every direction. Youssef threw himself to the ground like everyone else.

2

Maha couldn't tell how long she'd been lying on the ground in the dark. She knew that death was near and that it could swoop down at any moment. She thought of Luay, and of her parents and sister. She wished she could hear their voices one last time and say goodbye to them. But she didn't have her phone. It was in her purse, which had fallen to the ground when she had raced toward the altar. If only she'd had her purse, she could've used her earplugs! She thought of Youssef to whom she had not apologized. The church had been full when she'd arrived and the only empty place she'd found was in a pew in the far left-hand corner of the church. She'd looked around for Youssef during the service and was pretty sure that it was his head up near the front where the men traditionally sat, but she didn't see him again after the attack began. Had he managed to get past the altar and into the sacristy? Had they killed him? Was he lying somewhere on the ground like her, waiting for death to close in on him? She was still holding the rosary and she brought it up to her lips and kissed it. She would pray for her own deliverance, as well as Youssef's and that of the rest of the congregation. She would send her supplications to Our Lady of Deliverance who never abandoned those who sought her intercession. She said the prayer that she had read hundreds of times in the missal of the month of Mary and knew by heart:

Holy Mary, Pray for us. Holy Mother of God, Pray for us. Mother crucified, Mother sorrowful, Mother mournful, Mother afflicted, Mother forsaken, Mother desolate, Mother bereaved of thy Son, Mother transfixed with the sword, Mother consumed with grief, Mother filled with anguish, Mother crucified in heart, Mother most sad, Fountain of tears, Abyss of suffering, Rock of constancy, Anchor of confidence, Refuge of the forsaken, Shield of the oppressed, Subduer of the unbelieving, Comfort of the afflicted, Remedy of the sick, Strength of the weak, Harbor of the shipwrecked, Allayer of tempests, Terror of the treacherous, Treasure of the faithful, Eye of the Prophets, Staff of the Apostles, Crown of Martyrs, Light

of confessors, Consolation of widows, Joy of all Saints,
Pray for us, O Mother of Sorrows.

When she'd finished, she said six sets each of Our Father
and Hail Mary. In the middle of the seventh set, the blast from
two enormous explosions reverberated through the church
and the whole building shook; this was followed by volleys
of machine-gun fire and the sound of people screaming and
running. She expected to die any minute now but instead she
heard a voice shouting, "All those who are able to, get up, so
help you God!"

Maha didn't budge. She heard footsteps approaching and
then felt a hand shaking her. She tensed up with fear.

"Don't be frightened sister," a voice said. "We're your
Iraqi brothers."

She looked up and saw a heavily armed soldier wearing a
helmet with a small gadget attached to it that had a red flick-
ering light, which looked like a camera. He helped her up and,
holding her by the hand, accompanied her toward the vestibule of the church. Other men in the same kind of uniform
were also helping people out of the church.

In the courtyard, dozens of army soldiers bristling with
weapons and emergency paramedics with stretchers were
getting ready to enter the church and bring out the injured.
Ambulances and security vehicles were parked at the gate
where hundreds of onlookers gathered, crying and screaming.
Luay was among them but he didn't see her because he was
standing some way off. He had rushed to the church as soon
as he'd heard the news and stood outside with the rest of the
crowd. He'd asked to go in because his wife was in the church
and wasn't answering her mobile, but they told him no civil-
ians were allowed in.

Maha looked around and asked the soldier whose features
were easier to see now, "Where is Uncle Youssef?"

"Who's Youssef, miss?"

"He's my uncle, he was inside with us."

"We're going to bring everyone out," he reassured her. "Come this way."

He handed her over to one of the paramedics who asked her if she was wounded or if anything hurt.

"No, nothing," she told him. "I'm fine, I just I want to go home."

Maha had grayed in the span of a few hours. Her black hair was coated in a layer of white plaster dust that made her look like her mother.

That night, Maha sobbed as she washed her hair and scrubbed her blood-spattered legs in the bathroom.

She just couldn't stop crying.

3

Three days later, a correspondent for the Ishtar cable TV station contacted her to ask whether she would be willing to give an eyewitness account of the attack as part of a series that Ishtar TV was working on, entitled *Conversations with Survivors*. She was guarded initially and wanted to know how the man had obtained her phone number. When he replied that he was also a Christian and that the church had given him her number, she relaxed and agreed to his request. Luay tried to dissuade her from going ahead with the interview, saying that her appearance on television would cause them problems they could do without, and that going over what had happened that day would only upset her more and plunge her back into the nightmarish event, but she was determined to go ahead. She told him that she wanted the entire world to know the truth about that day.

She wore a long-sleeved black shirt, black pants, and a black headscarf. She looked pale, and her eyes were ringed by deep shadows. She was also squinting due to the powerful light the cameraman had set up on a tripod next to the camera. She sat on the leather armchair in the living room. The producer told Luay he could sit by her but he preferred not to appear in the footage and sat on a chair off to the side. The director of the program told her to speak naturally and spontaneously and he suggested she use colloquial Arabic—spectators would relate to it more easily than to the more formal language usually used on television. She gathered her courage, took a deep breath, and began. She had to stop several times to wipe away her tears but she said what she had to say, as she sat on her chair, holding a black-and-white photograph of Youssef in her hands.

4

My name is Maha George Haddad. I am a student at the University of Baghdad Medical School. I was one of the hostages at the Church of Our Lady of Deliverance on October 31, the day of the terrorist attack. My husband and I go to church every Sunday. It happened that he wasn't able to make it that day because he had a work commitment and couldn't get away. At about five-fifteen, the service was ending and everything had been fine until then. The pastor, Father Tha'ir, had just enjoined us to pray for peace in the country, for the formation of a new government, and for safety and security to prevail once again. Just as we began to recite Our Father we heard the sound of gunfire outside, but it wasn't very loud. Father Tha'ir reassured the congregation and we continued with the prayer, but the gunfire grew louder and more intense. The priest told the young men standing at the back to lock the main door. Suddenly there was a loud explosion that shook the building. The other priest, Father Waseem, started shouting and telling people to hurry to the priests' room behind the altar. People ran for cover helter-skelter. I too was afraid, and hurtled toward the altar, which was far from where I was. When I got there, the room was full of people, there wasn't an inch of space left, and there were people lying on the ground outside the doorway.

At that very moment, we heard shots being fired inside the church. They were really close and very loud. I threw myself to the ground behind the altar, covered my head with my arms and played dead. The terrorists had burst in suddenly and taken over the church, so easily and so quickly, it took just seconds. I found that really strange—how had they done it so easily?

I don't know exactly how many of them there were. Four men approached those of us at the far end of the church by the altar. I could tell from their accents that they were not Iraqis, except for the one closest to the altar. One of them was Syrian and I'm not sure about the other two—all I know, is that they didn't have Iraqi accents.

When they burst into the church, they began shooting at the people cowering on the ground on the far sides of the pews. Many were killed. The first person they gunned down right in front of my eyes was the deacon, Nabil. One of the terrorists came up to him and said something I didn't hear, but the deacon pushed him away. The man put a bullet in his head and he dropped to the ground. Standing on the side of the altar where the choir usually stood, Father Wasim tried to reason with them.

"Leave the worshippers alone. Deal with me! I'll give you whatever you want. Take me hostage even!"

They fired a bullet into his head. Then they shot Father Tha'ir, but he didn't die right away. He fell to the ground and kept repeating aloud, "Father, my spirit is in your hands." One of the men fired another two bullets into him and silenced him.

They were shooting randomly, at everything, but when they saw the cross, they went wild and began screaming, "Heathens! Nothing but heathens, worshipping the cross!"

They shot at the paintings above and on either side of the altar, and at the chandeliers, some of which came down. The Iraqi man was the one standing closest to me. I could hear the sound of the bullets as he fired. I was expecting him to kill me at any moment. Every time he fired his machine gun, the casings cascaded down on me. He'd fire and scream at the same time.

"O God, strengthen my faith! Forgive me, God, forgive me!"

They killed most of the men. They went into the priests' room behind the altar and threw in hand grenades; when they exploded we heard the sounds of moaning and crying.

One woman who was injured and was in agony begged the Iraqi man to kill her. "Don't let me suffer . . . please, kill me!" she said.

Do you know what he told her? "No, I'm going to let you suffer. Here and in the hellfire to which you're going."

She kept saying to him, "You're a coward, nothing but an infidel and a coward!"

He didn't shoot her but she eventually fell silent.

I expected to die with every passing second, I was sure he was going to shoot me in the legs or in the belly. I heard the guy with the Syrian accent say to the Iraqi, "Get one of the women up so she can come and talk on the phone."

I was praying as hard as I could, trying not to move and pretending to be dead. But he must have known I was still alive because he came over and kicked me.

"Get up," he yelled. "If you don't stand up right now, I'll shoot," he threatened.

I was terrified. I got up and went toward where the other guy was standing a few meters away. He gave me the mobile. He kept his weapon in full view so that I wouldn't forget his threat. He had the Baghdadiya TV station on the phone.

"Tell them you're one of the hostages, and that the Islamic State of Iraq says you must release our Muslim sisters in Egypt and our mujahideen brothers who are detained, or else we will all die. Tell them you're all fine."

I did as he said but I didn't say that we were all fine. When I was done, he took the phone from me and said, "Go on, get over there!" The church was littered with dead bodies and broken pews. I stepped back toward the Iraqi guy, but he raised his machine gun and yelled, "Get back there!" I did as I was told, and started praying the rosary.

Of course, I had no idea how much ammunition they had brought with them or how they had managed to get in with it all, but after a couple of hours, they had run out. The Iraqi said he only had four bullets left. One of the others answered him saying, "Use the hand grenades."

Every so often we would be shaken by a hand grenade they had thrown. A while later, one of them said it looked as if the army was preparing to storm the church. They agreed that when the troops came in, they would blow themselves up and kill everyone—us, them, and the soldiers outside. When I heard this, I was sure it was the end. We were all going to die.

I went on with my prayers and supplications. I lived by the grace of God and the Virgin Mary.

The lights were out because most of the chandeliers had fallen on top of us and in the last hour the power had been cut off. The church was shrouded in darkness, and it was difficult to see anything by the faint glimmer from one or two candles that were still burning at the altar. Then we heard the thud of loud explosions outside. It turned out that the Iraqi army had detonated stun grenades. One of the terrorists threw his remaining hand grenades inside the room where the third priest had hidden. And then it seems one of them blew himself up, and another one followed suit. The explosions were so loud that my ears were ringing; I couldn't hear anything. Only two men remained now, the Iraqi who was near me and another guy. The Iraqi was about four meters away and detonated the explosive belt strapped around his middle. I felt pieces of his flesh landing on my back and legs. I had covered my head with my hands and was begging God and the Virgin Mary to save me. Then the anti-terrorism squad entered the church and freed us.

But after what? After three-quarters of the people inside the church had died?

Our relative in whose house we were living was killed. May he rest in peace, this is his picture. A gentle, peaceful man, he didn't deserve this.

My question is why did they wait so long? If they'd mobilized earlier, they would've been able to rescue the people who were bleeding and shouldn't have died. There would've been far fewer casualties. I hold the Iraqi government wholly responsible for the slaughter. How were those people able to smuggle all that ammunition and those weapons through the checkpoints? Where was the safety and protection they keep promising us? There must have been some foul play at work, or at the least massive negligence. Or maybe our lives just aren't that valuable to them.

How long are we going to continue putting up with such a wretched situation? This is not the first attack against us Christians and I'm sorry to say it won't be the last. Even in my own family, it's the third attack. We were displaced from al-Dawra three years ago because of sectarian threats, and then had to leave our house a second time after an explosion, and we're now scattered between Ainkawa and Baghdad. We're being targeted. They are trying to make us leave this country. They accuse us of being 'Crusaders' and collaborators with the occupation. This is all baseless and a distortion of history. We didn't come here on tanks from the outside like all those people now playing at one-upmanship nationalism. Nobody has our back—not Iran, not Saudi Arabia, not America. The Americans haven't helped us; on the contrary, our situation has worsened.

At the end of the day, all we have is God and our faith. And no, we didn't come from outside. We've been here for centuries—everyone needs to hear this. History and archeology attest to it. Our monasteries and all the other archeological remains are there for all to see, not just in the north, but throughout Iraq. There are monasteries in Karbala and Nasiriya, and even in Najaf, where there are also the ruins of churches.

We've never had political ambitions. And we are not the ones looting, murdering, and firebombing places of worship. All we want is to live in peace. Our religion is one of peace.

That's all I have to say.

5

Youssef's body remained sprawled on the floor of the church for over four hours and it was only removed after all the hostages had been released and the wounded had been evacuated. All around him were human remains, pieces of broken glass and plaster, dust, and a small pool of blood that had been seeping from his body. One of the paratroopers from the counter-terrorism unit that had stormed the church stepped on his left hand by mistake crushing the bones on three of his fingers. The man was holding a small camera and filming the operation, and he kept telling the hostages to look at the camera as they thanked God for their safety. A few days later, he uploaded the footage to YouTube, including some information about the officer who led the operation and patriotic songs in praise of the Golden Unit that had rescued the hostages.

Youssef's corpse didn't appear in the footage. He felt no pain when his fingers were crushed. One of the four bullets that had entered his body hours earlier had found its way to his heart and silenced it. Seconds before, his lips had whispered "ya Maryam" but he never finished the prayer. His eyes remained open even as they sank into the shadows of death.

Selected Hoopoe Titles

No Knives in the Kitchens of This City
by Khaled Khalifa, translated by Leri Price

No Road to Paradise
by Hassan Daoud, translated by Marilyn Booth

Embrace on Brooklyn Bridge
by Ezzedine C. Fishere, translated by John Peate

*

hoopoe is an imprint for engaged, open-minded readers hungry for outstanding fiction that challenges headlines, re-imagines histories, and celebrates original storytelling. Through elegant paperback and digital editions, **hoopoe** champions bold, contemporary writers from across the Middle East alongside some of the finest, groundbreaking authors of earlier generations.

At hoopoefiction.com, curious and adventurous readers from around the world will find new writing, interviews, and criticism from our authors, translators, and editors.